# Sylvia's Journey

Leah Brewer

In memory of Alvin Elton Castleberry. I'll never forget you, dear brother.

# Author's Note

Nearly three years ago, I embarked on a deeply personal mission to bring the first installment of this series, Keatyn's Journey, to life. Writing the second novel, Sylvia's Journey, brought me immense joy as it allowed me to fondly remember my late brother, Alvin.

Since the release of this series, I faced the painful reality of losing my beloved cover model from Keatyn's Journey, Samantha. She was a radiant spirit whose light shone brightly, bringing joy to everyone around her. I cherished her deeply, and her absence is profoundly felt every day by all who loved her.

In her honor, I made the decision to revisit and revise the books in this series to make them the best they can be. Thank you to everyone who took the time to read and review the books. Your insightful comments have been invaluable in shaping these revisions. May God bless you all!

# Chapter 1

What if Sylvia Mason's husband was still alive? As she stepped through the courthouse doors, the weight of the question pressed on her mind, the same question she'd pondered a thousand times before.

With each stride into the gathering dusk, the warm night air enveloped her, carrying the faint hum of distant traffic.

She could still picture Lee jogging up to her at this exact spot. One day he'd been here, the next day she was a widow.

Two years ago, the chief of police told Sylvia Lee had been killed in the line of duty as an undercover police officer. The only thing left at the scene was a pile of Lee's blood and a bullet shell.

Even though they never located his body, the coroner concluded he wouldn't have survived the loss of so much blood. Everyone thought his body had been dumped in Pensacola Bay, but there was no proof.

She'd considered using her savings to hire a team of divers. If she could only find his body, perhaps the guilt of having feelings for someone else wouldn't be so hard to deal with.

Would she ever find closure? If they found Lee, would her feelings for Alvin Griffin go away? Alvin. The man had stuck by her side through every hardship since Lee died. Yet she pushed him away every chance she got.

All she had to do was make it down the steps and to her car. Then, she could breathe after an exhausting day at court. Her feet throbbed, and she couldn't wait to get out of her three-inch heels. As a shorter-than-average bi-racial woman working as the prosecuting attorney, wearing heels boosted her self-confidence.

She furrowed her brow, her lips pressing into a thin line of concern. The thought of prosecuting a young woman for taking someone's life while distracted by her phone was far from what she had envisioned for her career. Yet, this heavy responsibility had consumed her every waking moment for the past few weeks.

As she slid behind the wheel of her white Lexus RX350, the smooth leather seats enveloped her in comfort. She glanced in the rearview mirror just in time to see a black Tahoe merge into the lane directly behind her.

After navigating through the familiar streets of her neighborhood, she finally turned into her driveway and parked in the spacious garage. As she closed the car door, her brow furrowed in concern.

The black Tahoe lingered on the opposite side of the road, just a couple of houses down. The vehicle's dark tint made it difficult to discern who might be inside, but for some reason a flicker of unease sparked within her.

Despite a lingering sense of unease creeping over her, she took a deep breath and closed the garage door. The sound of it clanking into place echoed through the dim space.

She stepped into the stillness of her home, the air thick with an unsettling quiet. The faint glow from the lamp in the living room provided ample light, illuminating the abandoned toys her boys had left scattered around.

Her parents had taken them to their house in Milton for a sleepover, leaving the house enveloped in an unusual silence that felt both comforting and eerie.

She meandered through the hallway, the floorboards creaking softly beneath her weight, as she tried to shake off the strange sensation that made her feel as though she were not alone.

The song "Blown Away" by Carrie Underwood played a loop in her mind as she turned the shower on. She pulled up her phone's music app and shuffled her bedtime playlist.

Music had been her safe place since Lee died. It helped her mind focus on something else, even for a few minutes.

A creaking sound caused Sylvia to jerk her head sideways and scan her bedroom. Thankfully, no one was there.

She blew out her breath. First the Tahoe made her suspicious and now this. After making a mental note to slow down on the true crime mystery shows, she laid her phone on the counter.

It's not like someone would be in the house with her. Right?

Her refrigerator chose that moment to kick into high gear, and she swallowed down a scream that turned into a laugh as she chided herself for acting like a silly, scaredy cat.

Narrowing her eyes, she cocked her head to stare out the bathroom door.

Was that a shadow?

The hair on her arms stood up.

She grabbed her phone and dialed her mom's number before turning the shower off.

Mom picked up on the second ring. "Hi, honey. The boys and I were just talking about you."

Sylvia threw a few necessities in her overnight bag as she talked. "Hey, mom. This last case has me on edge. I'm heading over there."

"Is everything all right?" The concern in Mom's voice caused Sylvia's heart to thump harder and faster.

Her eyes darted out the bedroom door. Nothing seemed to be out of place. Still, she speed-walked through the back door and jumped into her car before answering. "I'm a little bit lonely."

With trembling hands, she stuck the keys in the ignition and gunned it, backing out of the driveway sideways.

"Sylvia?" Her mom's voice came through the Bluetooth car speaker. "What's happening? It sounds like you're breathing heavily."

"Mom, I'm fine."  Sylvia's breathing leveled out the further she got from the house. "I'm on edge after the past few weeks."

"Okay, honey, we'll get your room ready. Do you want to stay on the phone with me?"

Sylvia clicked the blinker to turn onto the main road. "No, that's okay. I'm going to listen to some music."

"Well, all right then. See you in a bit." Mom said.

"See you shortly." Sylvia ended the call and turned the radio on to classical music to calm her nerves.

She took a moment to steady herself, inhaling deeply as the tension in her chest rose. Glancing into the rearview mirror, she blinked rapidly, trying to dispel the growing sense of unease that enveloped her.

A shiver coursed down her spine. She had no doubt the same black Tahoe from before lingered behind her, its headlights cutting through the dusk like unblinking eyes.

And it was getting closer by the second.

# Chapter 2

Sylvia swerved into the passing lane and pressed the accelerator all the way down. The Tahoe followed suit. Normally, she would appreciate the sight of the palm trees lining the road, but not today.

Right now, her only goal was to shake off the Tahoe.

Her eyes flicked between the road and the rearview mirror. The traffic light ahead turned green for a left turn. She quickly jerked the wheel and did a U-turn, speeding away in the opposite direction.

She picked up her phone to call the police, but it slipped out of her hand and landed on the passenger floorboard. Her eyes darted to the phone, which was too far over to reach and keep her hands on the wheel.

The police station was nearby, and that's where she wanted to go. She looked at the cars behind her and sighed. There was a Jeep and two smaller cars, but no Tahoe. Sylvia shook her head, wondering why she hadn't used her Bluetooth to call the police. She didn't want to make that mistake again.

What if someone was following her?

She rubbed her sweaty palms on her sweatpants as she passed the police station. Now that she felt safe, her shoulders relaxed.

For the second time that night, Sylvia chuckled at her paranoia. Yet in the back of her mind, the question lingered, was she being paranoid? It was too big a coincidence for the exact vehicle to keep coming around. She'd have to keep her eyes open.

What if the person who killed Lee believed she was a loose end? That couldn't be the case, though. Why would they wait two years? It must be the lack of closure causing these thoughts.

Since becoming a Christian, she had experienced more peace than ever, so what was lacking? The truth about Lee's death. How could she find peace until she discovered what had happened?

Thirty minutes later, she drove past the Welcome to Milton sign and turned off Main Street onto Lakeshore Drive. The third house on the quiet street was a Mid-Century home her mother remodeled when Sylvia had been in high school.

Sylvia walked in and locked the door behind her. She dropped her bag on the sofa and glanced toward the backyard, which was easily visible thanks to the large glass wall that slid open in the middle.

Edgar Engle, her dad, flipped a steak on the grill, while her mom and the boys were enjoying the heated swimming pool.

She stepped outside and elbowed dad in the ribs. "Well, I'm kinda offended I didn't get an invite."

Smiling, dad continued cutting red bell peppers on the tray for grilling. "You're always welcome here, little girl. You don't need an invite."

Jane, her mom raised her voice. "We were hoping you'd be forced to go on a date with your handsome friend, Alvin."

Mom had met Alvin one day when he stopped by the park to say hi to the boys, and she'd been on Sylvia to give him a chance ever since.

Sylvia covered her flushed cheeks with her hands. "Oh, mom. I'd much rather be here eating dad's steak."

"Is that your excuse today, my dear?" Mom asked as she stepped out of the pool.

Sylvia was always amazed at how her mother didn't seem to age. Her mom's dark brown skin had a healthy sheen, and she was more muscular than Sylvia had ever been.

"If I didn't know any better, I'd swear you found the Fountain of Youth," Sylvia said, swiping a slice of red bell pepper and popping it into her mouth.

Dad's eyes brightened. "And I get to be married to her." He rubbed the slight pudge in his belly and smiled.

Edgar and Jane were opposites when it came to looks. She was dark and exotic, while he was pale and favored Bill Gates. But they had been happily married since their early twenties. Sylvia always called them her own set of David Bowie and Iman parents.

Mom flexed her muscles, and Sylvia lost it. After her laughter died down, she cocked her head at her dad. "Why are you grilling so late? Didn't you all have dinner?"

He emptied a bowl of vegetables on the grill. "We had a late lunch on the boat. By the time we got home, the boys wanted one of my steaks, so here we are. There's plenty if you're hungry."

She breathed in the tangy seasonings on the sizzling steak and licked her lips. "I sure am."

"Come swim with us, mom." Oakland's voice turned to a screech right before Rhyland dunked him under the water.

Oakland surfaced and sprayed Rhyland with water from his brown curly hair. Oakland's hair hung past his shoulders while Rhyland kept his cut shorter.

After their swim and steak, they cleaned up, and Sylvia kissed everyone goodnight. "I love y'all. I'm about to pass out. Boys, let's say our prayers before y'all go to your room."

"Okay, mama." The boys pushed each other into the wall as they ran down the hallway. Rhyland put his foot out, and Oakland tripped over it, knocking his head right into Rhyland's elbow.

Sylvia curled up in bed after tending to Oakland and helping Rhyland feel better. Rhyland had been upset about hurting his twin and had pouted more than Oakland. Afterward, they said their prayers, brushed their teeth, and she changed into her pajamas.

Not long after she drifted off to sleep, a vivid dream enveloped her. In it, she spotted Lee alive. But just as she began to run toward him, a black Tahoe barreled down the street, striking him down.

With a start, she awoke, her heart racing and sweat beading on her brow. The nightmare clung to her, and as she brushed away the tears streaming down her cheeks, a fierce determination settled within her. She vowed to uncover the truth behind her husband's fate.

# Chapter 3

The fragrance of cocoa and butter filled the air. Sylvia closed her eyes, savoring the chocolate goodness as she made her way into the kitchen.

Sylvia kissed Dad's cheek. "Good Sunday morning."

He folded the newspaper and placed it on the table. "Good morning, sweetheart." His lips turned downward. "The paper reports that the verdict should come in tomorrow regarding the case you've been working on."

"Yes, I truly hope so," she murmured, her gaze distant as if lost in thought.

"I came across an article stating that Antonio Morales is considered a criminal. What's your perspective on him?"

"When I see Antonio Morales, all I see is a father drowning in sorrow."

Mom smiled as she whisked a pan of chocolate gravy. "Did you sleep well?" Anytime a conversation went in a direction she didn't like, she tended to change the subject.

"I did. I was worn out. Thank you both for taking us out fishing yesterday. I haven't had such a peaceful Saturday in ages."

She peeked over her mom's shoulder and gawked at the stove. "Are you making chocolate gravy?"

Her mom grinned. "I sure am."

"Smells delicious. How can I help?"

Turning the burner low, Mom swapped the whisk for a spoon. "You can set the table, then grab the boys."

Sylvia poured half a cup of black coffee and headed down the hall.

After breakfast, Sylvia zipped her bag and looked into Mom's eyes. "Would you and Dad want to come to church with us this morning?"

After a deep frown, Mom jumped up from the kitchen table. "You know I'm not much on going to church, Sylvia. You know how people treated us after we married."

Sylvia cast a glance down at her feet. "I only invite you because I love you, Mom. Keatyn cared enough about my soul to invite me, and I want to do the same for you and Dad."

The empty coffee cup in Mom's hand landed on the table with a loud thump. "I've already told you God abandoned me when I needed Him the most."

Sylvia closed her eyes and took a breath. "I'm sorry you went through that, Mom. But look where you are now. You're an amazing, strong woman. You think you did all this without God's help?"

She scoffed. "I had your dad's help, and he had mine. Without your dad, I'd be dead by my own hand."

Mom's high school sweetheart murdered her parents while she was away at college. All because they wouldn't allow him to marry her. He got drunk and went to their home one night, killing them in their sleep.

Two days later, her only living grandparent died of a heart attack. Mom dealt with losing her parents, a fiancé, and her grandmother while attending college.

Her mom and dad were college classmates and friends. He'd been there for her and her sister, seeing them through their grief. Mom blamed herself and contemplated suicide on more than one occasion, but Dad had always talked her through her spells of self-hatred and blame.

They married the following year. After going to church once they never returned.

Mom said that the people blamed her for her parents' murder, and they didn't accept the marriage between a white man and a black woman. She felt that no one seemed to be happy for them.

Sylvia kept her voice low and even. "Since becoming a Christian, I've never been more at peace." Sylvia reached for her mom's hand. "I would love for you to feel the peace, I do. And I know you can do it with God's help."

"Please stop pressuring me to do something I don't want to do. I would never do this to you."

Tears burned Sylvia's eyes. "Oh, Mom."

Oakland and Rhyland bounced out of their bedroom and started wrestling. Rhyland tripped, fell on the sofa table, and busted his lip.

Sylvia hurried into the bathroom and came back with the first aid kit.

No surprise, Mom had left the room.

Disappointment crashed into Sylvia's ribcage. She'd been trying to get her parents to come to church for months with no luck.

Sylvia remembered the day Keatyn invited her, and she smiled. She had no idea how much her life would change by saying yes. A few months after she started attending, Sylvia became a Christian. This was the best decision she ever made. Even though she lost Lee, she felt lighter. She started to react to things differently and experienced true joy for the first time. She wanted the same for her parents.

BREAK

Later that morning, Rhyland skipped into the Fort Hill Church of Christ and went straight to Alvin Griffin in the auditorium.

Alvin, with his striking dark blonde hair and sapphire blue eyes. When he smiled, his straight white teeth enhanced his handsome features. A former Navy SEAL, he certainly looked the part. He had left the Navy the previous year due to an injury to his leg. Although the injury resulted in a slight limp, it was difficult to notice unless you were aware of it.

"Whatcha doing?" Rhyland asked Alvin.

Alvin glanced up from the papers he'd been reading. "Getting ready to teach Bible class. What're you doing?"

Rhyland put his hand on his hip. "I'm ready to go see Mrs. Keatyn. She's teaching us about Joseph's coat of many colors."

Alvin ruffled Rhyland's hair as Sylvia and Oakland walked down the aisle. "Good morning, Sylvia."

Sylvia swallowed and met Alvin's gaze. The teal maxi dress and white short-sleeved sweater she had thought made her skin glow seemed poised to suffocate her. "Morning, Alvin. How are you?"

"Doing well." He examined the papers in his hand. "Putting my thoughts together before class."

Gareth Davenport, the preacher, stopped by to shake Sylvia's hand. Sylvia chuckled at the thought of how Gareth was now married to her best friend, Keatyn, who was also Alvin's sister. Keatyn had once struggled with her feelings for Gareth, insisting that ministers were supposed to be old and unattractive. However, Gareth defied that stereotype with his deep dimples, black hair, and captivating eyes that made hearts skip a beat.

"Good morning, Sylvia, Rhyland, and Oakland." Gareth pointed at his daughter. "Lily is waiting on you two boys to go to class."

"Can we go, mama?" Oakland asked.

"Go ahead. But no running." Sylvia pushed a long, dark curl behind her ear before looking back at Alvin. "You're teaching this quarter?"

Alvin's eyes followed Gareth as he continued down the aisle, greeting church members. "I am."

"That's wonderful." She took a step toward him. "I'm looking forward to class."

Alvin chuckled. "Let's wait until after the class is over before saying it's wonderful."

Sylvia squeezed his hand and lowered her voice. "You'll do great."

His voice was sharp, almost like he had something more on his mind. "I better get up there. Thanks for the encouragement."

Sylvia pressed her lips together. She didn't blame Alvin for snapping at her. She'd not given him a reason to be nice. Not really. "Sure."

Alvin's eyes landed on the floor. "I'm sorry. I didn't mean to sound so hateful."

"It's all right. I know you're nervous." She took her seat.

Rebecca VanHouten, another friend, slid into the seat next to Sylvia and raised a fan to cover her mouth. She leaned close to Sylvia and whispered, "Alvin has a date with a girl named Brinley tonight."

Sylvia's heart dropped. "A date?"

"Yes. Apparently, with a friend of Cordelia's granddaughter." Rebecca lowered her voice. "I thought you should know. If you want Alvin, you better say so before he's no longer available."

Sylvia looked composed on the outside, but her insides churned like a bucket of butter. Rebecca's words hit too close to home. If she wanted to pursue something with Alvin, time was running out.

Alvin said they were starting a study on 2 Samuel chapter 22, but her mind wandered. Determined to push all feelings aside, she cleared her throat and focused on the lesson.

# Chapter 4

After three hours, the jury found Sydney Clark guilty of Vehicular Manslaughter. She would serve a year, two at the most. But poor Evangeline Morales would never have another chance at life.

Sylvia couldn't stop the wave of relief as she walked out of the courthouse. Shuffling through her purse for her sunglasses, she groaned. Finally, her hand wrapped around the case, and she slipped on her Ray-Bans.

A red Ford Taurus slowed, and a man blew a slow whistle. She ignored him as she waved at two police officers.

Sobbing came from behind her. As she turned to see who it was, a flash of hands came at her, connecting with her cheek.

Sylvia's head snapped sideways from the unexpected blow, and her Ray-Bans flew off her face.

The defendant's mother, Maria Clark, let out a cry and wrapped her hand around the bun atop Sylvia's head. "You ruined Sydney's life!"

After dropping her bag to the ground, Sylvia dug her fingernails into Maria's chin and jerked her face sideways. Maria let out a screech and tried to bite Sylvia's arm.

Sylvia punched Maria on the side of her face.

It didn't seem to faze the crazed woman.

She rammed her head into Sylvia's shoulder, burying her hand in Sylvia's hair.

As Sylvia lost her footing, her knee slammed into the concrete step. Squealing, she grasped Maria's bony arm, squeezing as hard as possible.

Maria landed on the concrete by Sylvia and piled on top of her. Sylvia raised her forearms and wiggled her right leg out from under Maria.

By then, both police officers had made it up the steps. The taller one wrapped his arms around Maria, pulling her away from Sylvia and down the courthouse steps.

Sylvia rubbed the side of her head and tucked a long, dark hair behind her ear. More strands lay balled up in Maria's bony hand.

The last thing Sylvia expected was to be attacked by the defendant's mother. The woman had sat in the courtroom dressed to kill, looking like a flea market version of Sarah Jessica Parker during the trial. She'd hung on every word and taken notes as Sylvia built a case to prosecute Sydney Clark.

Sydney had emulated her mother's attitude during the trial. At one point, she looked so bored as she played with her fingernails while the only witness testified. Her best friend, LeAnne Ewing, said she'd asked Sydney to stop texting while behind the wheel.

Maria's hands dropped to her sides, and her lips trembled. "My baby girl's going to prison."

A few hours after giving her statement at the police station, Sylvia lay sprawled on her cream sofa with an ice pack on her cheek. She questioned her sanity for dropping the charges against Maria Clark as she flipped through the channels on her TV. Local reporters Jack Gregory and Victoria Evans appeared on the screen.

Victoria began the report by stating, "Nineteen-year-old Sydney Clark was found guilty of involuntary manslaughter today and sentenced to three years in connection with the death of Evangeline Morales. Clark, a resident of Pensacola, lost control of her Camry and crossed into oncoming traffic, resulting in the death of Ms. Morales. The investigation revealed that Clark was responding to a text message from a friend at the time of the accident. Morales was the daughter of businessman Antonio Morales."

Jack continued with his lips pressed into a thin line. "It's a sad case, indeed. Things became complicated as Prosecutor Mason left the courthouse today."

Victoria nodded her head. "Absolutely. The defendant's mother, Maria Clark, physically attacked Prosecutor Sylvia Mason."

A photo of herself and Maria on the ground appeared in the right corner of the screen. Unable to find the remote, Sylvia sprang off the sofa and turned the TV off. She pursed her lips. Who had been taking photos?

She grabbed the ice pack and gently laid it on her cheekbone before walking to the window. She peered through the blinds, and her face lit up. The sky shined bright orange and pink, quickly fading to dark blue. Such beauty! It reminded her of the day she decided to become a prosecutor.

Twelve-year-old Sylvia and the kids from her neighborhood had been outside when the group bully got mad and jumped on the smallest kid. Before they were able to get him off the kid, he'd managed to bloody his nose and break his glasses. The bully's mama had blamed the other kid. Sylvia had looked up at the colorful sky and decided then and there that she would grow up to ensure people paid for doing wrong. Unfortunately, some of the cases she'd prosecuted had not been the cases she had in mind.

Before she lowered the blinds she caught a glimpse of a black Tahoe creeping by her house.

Heat traveled up her neck. She burst through the front door, ready to confront whoever was behind the wheel.

# Chapter 5

The Tahoe zipped away, leaving Sylvia standing in her front yard in her pajamas. She would call the police, but for what? Nothing illegal had been done.

She slipped inside and padded to the kitchen, hoping to find a brownie. Mom had asked if the boys could have another sleepover after the incident with Maria Clark. She figured Sylvia needed her rest. And she was right.

She twisted the wedding ring she'd been unable to take off around her finger as her mom's words played in her mind.

*"Your boys need a father, Sylvia."*

*"You can't spend the rest of your life alone, Sylvia."*

*"That young man, Alvin, sure is handsome, Sylvia."*

*"Don't you want to have someone to love, Sylvia?"*

Maybe she should see if Alvin could grab a quick bite.

Fortunately, a knock at the door interrupted her train of thought. When she opened the door, she found Alvin's sister, Keatyn Davenport, standing on the other side. With her fit physique, sandy blonde hair, and striking turquoise eyes, Keatyn reminded Sylvia of an old-school Wonder Woman with lighter hair.

Keatyn rushed past Sylvia. "I knew it! I told Gareth you'd be sitting here alone in your pajamas. And I was right."

Sylvia groaned. "I'm not sitting here alone."

Keatyn peeked into the kitchen area. "Is there someone here I don't know about?"

"Of course not. I meant I was literally about to call Alvin."

Keatyn clapped her hands together and squealed. "You were?"

"Don't go getting the wrong idea." Sylvia scrunched her nose. "It's dinner. Nothing deep."

"Sureeeee." Keatyn drew the word out before tugging her tennis shoes off and sinking onto the sofa. "You know I would love for you to give Alvin a chance, but he's out bowling with Kyle."

"I'm hungry. But I don't necessarily want to get out." Sylvia massaged the back of her neck. "I'm mentally drained after today."

"Considering that shiner, you're probably physically drained as well." Keatyn grimaced. "I still can't believe that woman attacked you."

Sylvia touched her cheekbone and winced. "That makes two of us."

"Well, guess what? Rebecca's on her way over with a large order of fish tacos." Keatyn licked her lips. "And a shrimp boat."

"That sounds amazing." Sylvia lowered herself into the recliner. Only to raise and toss a Superman action figure into a basket by the couch. Rubbing her side, she glanced at Keatyn. "But what about Gareth?"

"Gareth is working on his Sunday sermon. Daddy and Cordelia are taking the kids to Chuckee Cheese. So, Rebecca and I are all yours."

Within the hour, Sylvia and her friends gathered around her dining room table with the food Rebecca had brought.  Sylvia chomped on a piece of shrimp. "Rebecca knows the way to my heart."

Keatyn howled. "At least somebody does. I didn't think anybody could get through the stone around it...miss uptight prosecutor."

Trying not to laugh, Sylvia cocked her head and raised her brows. "You think I'm uptight, do you there, Miss Keatyn I'll never date a preacher, Davenport?"

Shrugging, Keatyn forked a giant shrimp and dipped it in cocktail sauce. "What do you think, Rebecca?"

Rebecca shook her finger at Keatyn. "Oh no, you don't. I'm not getting into the debate on Sylvia and Alvin's love life."

Brushing a piece of flaxen blonde hair out of her mouth, Rebecca's eyes lit up. "You should've seen Keatyn's face the first time we ran into Gareth over dinner. I thought she was going to pass out when I suggested she join him when I had to go check on Bliss."

Keatyn let out a cackle. "You caught me off guard."

Rebecca cut three pieces of pie and plopped down on a bean bag by the sofa. "I knew y'all were meant to be as soon as I saw the look on your face."

Keatyn groaned and shoveled in a bite of pie. "Just like Sylvia and Alvin."

Sylvia glanced at the pie, and her stomach flopped. "I need to do something first."

Rebecca glanced up at Sylvia. "What's that?"

"I need to see if I can find Lee's body. I'm going to hire a team of divers next week."

# Chapter 6

Later in the week, Sylvia poured a cup of coffee as she waited for the boys to come to breakfast. A few rumbles of thunder echoed in the distance, causing her to jump and spill coffee on the quartz countertop in her kitchen.

Fortunately, the coffee didn't spill on the white tile. She wiped the counter before raising the kitchen blinds. Rain hammered against the windows so hard she couldn't even see the swing set in the backyard.

She took stock of her skirt and high heels and tapped her chin. Today would be a good day to wear a pantsuit. She headed to her bedroom to change.

A few minutes later, she returned to the kitchen wearing a solid gray pair of slacks, a mauve top, and beige loafers. The gray wasn't her favorite color against her tan skin, but the mauve top matched her brown eyes perfectly. She hung rain jackets for herself and the boys by the garage door.

Oakland barreled into the room. "Can we leave now?"

Rhyland pushed his glass of Orange Juice across the dining room table with his pencil. The glass vibrated on the wood like it could tip over any second.

Sylvia raised her left eyebrow. "Drink your juice, Rhyland."

"Yes, ma'am." He drained the juice in one gulp before shoving his pencil and papers in his backpack.

A few minutes later, as Sylvia backed into the heavy rain, her heart softened. Rhyland declared he was the meteorologist and Oakland was his cameraman. She loved how her boys could turn something like the weather into a game, even though that same weather made the drive to school twice as long as usual.

Finally, Sylvia pulled under the overhanging. "I love you, boys."

"Love you!" The boys scampered out of the car. Sylvia waved at the teacher, Mrs. Ellis, as she shuffled the boys into the building before turning her attention to the next set of kids walking up the sidewalk.

After waiting for what seemed like forever in traffic, she pulled onto a back road. Hoping to miss the morning rush, she headed toward her office downtown.

The car speaker belted out a ring, and her eyes darted to the dashboard screen.

"Hello." She kept her eyes glued to the wet road.

"Sylvia? Dad and I wanted to say good morning."

"Morning."

"Dad's getting his eyes checked at eleven today. Would you like to meet us for lunch?"

"I can do that."

"How about we meet at one? At Tia's Tacos?"

"Sounds good." Sylvia stopped at a stop sign.

Immediately after she stopped, metal hitting metal caused her teeth to chatter. Her body rose out of her seat and into the seatbelt, causing the belt to dig into her neck.

"What was that sound?"

Sylvia drew in a sharp breath and ran her hand over her neck. "I got rear-ended."

"Are you hurt?"

"I'm fine. But I need to get off here and handle this."

"Be careful. Dad and I love you."

Dad muttered something Sylvia couldn't make out.

Mom answered whatever he said. "Ed, she's fine. Sounds like it's a simple fender bender."

"I'll see y'all at lunch. Be safe driving in."

Sylvia clicked the button on her steering wheel to end the call and gaped at a small cut below her thumb. She looked around for what could've cut her, but nothing came to mind. It wasn't a significant cut, so it would be better to deal with it later.

She covered her thumb with a napkin and stepped out of the SUV. A tall, dark-haired man sheltered from the rain with an umbrella leaned against her vehicle.

As she approached, he raised his hand and spoke loudly, his thick accent overpowering the sound of the weather. "I'm sorry; my brakes didn't work on the slick road."

Sylvia shook her head and raised her voice. "I understand."

"Have you already called the police?" The man stepped back, letting his eyes rest on her face.

A bout of wind caught her umbrella, and she had to hold tight to keep it from blowing out of her hands. "Not yet. Why don't you get back in your vehicle, and I'll call from my car?"

The man's eyes twitched. "Good idea."

Sylvia turned, and a hundred daddy long-legs seemed to crawl down her neck. The man drove a black Tahoe, like the one sitting in front of her house.

She met his gaze, and her mouth went dry as recognition lit up her eyes. The dark hair. The nose slightly too large for his face. He had been in the courtroom during the trial against Sydney Clark.

"I'll be right back." She wanted to run. Or scream. But instead, she slowly backed away from him.

The man smiled, revealing teeth so white they had to be veneered.

Sylvia's feet hit the wet pavement, making her gray slacks cling to her legs. Ignoring the discomfort, she sighed in relief as her hand grasped the door handle.

Those daddy long-legs moved to her scalp, starting at her hair particles. She pulled on the door handle and whirled around to make sure the man was still at the back of the car. To make herself feel better.

It didn't work.

The man stood so close she could've smelled his breath if not for the rain.

Sylvia opened her mouth. To speak or maybe to scream but didn't get the chance. He slammed his fist into her temple.

A sharp throbbing exploded in her brow, and her legs gave out. The man caught her and carried her to the Tahoe.

Searing pain racked her skull as she squeezed her eyes shut, praying it was all just a bad dream.

The movement when the Tahoe drove through the stop sign caused Sylvia's intestines to twist into painful knots. Spasms racked her stomach, and she clamped her lips together. It was no use. Leaning over the seat, she emptied her stomach onto the carpet.

Oddly, her only thought was that she'd hate to be the one cleaning the carpets.

# Chapter 7

The warm, inviting scent of cinnamon and ripe apple filled the air, wrapping around Sylvia like a cozy blanket as she rolled over in bed. She squinted against the light, her fingers tangling in her hair as she rubbed the back of her head. A jarring pain shot through her, beginning at the base of her neck and creeping upward, like a tight knot tightening at her scalp.

Despite the pain, she had to figure out what the smell was. It reminded her of the last Thanksgiving with Lee when he baked an apple pie that had a bit too much cinnamon.

She opened her eyes to find an ornate armoire with a large television on the top shelf at the foot of her bed. After blinking a few times, the same armoire and television remained in view. The room was eerily quiet and unfamiliar.

Working past the throb in her head, an onslaught of memories surfaced.

The storm.

The wreck.

The man.

She threw the covers back and hobbled to the window. A full moon bathed the garden below in an effervescent glow. Trees lined the distance like she was in the middle of the woods.

Turning her attention to the room, she walked back to the bed. The bedding consisted of silk sheets, a luxury comforter, and a soft leopard throw draped across the foot of the bed. Fluffy designer pillows lay scattered about the bed. Beside the bed, she found a Glade plug-in to be the source of the cinnamon and apples.

One of the doors opened to a bathroom and closet. The massive closet could've been another bedroom with clothes and shoes. That meant the other door had to lead to freedom.

She hoped.

The doorknob turned, and Sylvia hurried inside the bathroom, clicking the lock in place.

"Hello?" A woman's singsong voice rang from the bedroom. "Are you in the restroom, Señorita?"

Against her better judgment, she jerked the door open and rushed into the bedroom. A short, stocky, dark-skinned woman stood there. "Who are you?"

The woman's full lips curved up at the corners. "I am Señora Louise Estrada." She bent down in a curtsy before continuing. "I've been brought here from Cuba to care for you."

Sylvia scrunched her eyebrows and twisted her lips. "Why? Brought where? To Pensacola? I don't understand."

Louise handed Sylvia two Tylenol and a bottle of Dasani. "The cook prepared enchiladas for dinner and pecan pie for dessert. I'm sure you are hungry."

Sylvia inspected the pills. "No, I want to leave." Satisfied they were Tylenol, she popped them in her mouth, washing them down with a gulp of water before marching past Louise.

Louise grabbed Sylvia's arm, stopping her in her tracks. "You are to stay here. I will take care of you."

Sylvia laid her eyes on her arm before meeting Louise's gaze. "I don't need anyone to care for me. I'm perfectly capable of taking care of myself."

Capable? Sure. But at the moment, she wanted to lay her head on a heating pad and cry herself to sleep.

To be so short, the woman had some power behind her grip. Her grip loosened, but her tone was firm. "You cannot leave this place."

Sylvia's spine tensed. "What do you mean?"

"You must stay here." Louise wrung her hands and moved closer to the door. "It's for your own protection."

Sylvia met Louise's eyes and sensed the woman was sincere. But why, she didn't know. "Protection from what?"

Louise shook her head back and forth. "My employer has instructed me not to engage you in this conversation. Now, make yourself comfortable while I go get your dinner."

"I don't want dinner." She put both hands under her chin like a steeple. "I want to go home. Please."

Louise walked out and locked the door behind her. Sylvia noticed the sound and tried the doorknob, but it wouldn't open. She leaned against the door and kicked it, stopping only when pain shot through her calf.

She limped over to the bed and held her tingling nose. She would not cry. She had to be strong to escape whatever mess she was in. To get home to the boys.

Less than ten minutes later, Louise walked back into the room carrying a tray and clicked her tongue. "What are you trying to do? Hurt yourself? I could hear that racket all the way down in the kitchen."

Sylvia narrowed her eyes. "I don't like being locked up. Let me go."

Louise's dark eyes flashed with sympathy. "I am very sorry. But I promise it is for your own good." She put the tray of food and an ice pack on the bed.

Trying her best to ignore the spices in the air, Sylvia sat down on the bed and placed the ice pack on her heel. "That makes no sense. Who's keeping me locked up?" Sylvia glanced at the food, and her traitor of a stomach growled.

Louise lowered her voice to a slight whisper. "You already know it's your father."

"My father?" Sylvia screeched. "Where is he? And where's my mother?"

The color drained from Louise's face, and she slowly backed away from Sylvia. "Your father was right. You've lost your senses."

"My father would never have me locked up. Ever." Sylvia's vision clouded, and she ground her teeth. "I suggest you tell whomever this person is that I want to see them. Now."

"Yes, Miss Evangeline," Louise said as she slipped out the door, clicking the lock behind her.

# Chapter 8

Sylvia catapulted off the bed and pulled on the doorknob. Her stomach churned as it had in the vehicle. "My name is NOT Evangeline!" She called out and beat against the door until her throat was raw and her hands were numb.

Her mind raced as she made her way back to the bed.

Evangeline? How anyone could mistake Sylvia for someone named Evangeline was beyond her. This had to be a big misunderstanding.

Considering she was not in immediate physical danger, she glanced at the food.

Her stomach rumbled loudly, like an old muscle car without a muffler. It had been at least ten hours since she had eaten. The last thing she remembered was dropping the boys off at school.

She needed to eat to maintain her strength in order to escape this place. If they had wanted to kill her, they would have done it by now.

With her mind made up, Sylvia bowed her head and prayed, "Dear Lord, thank You for my family, friends, and church community, and especially for Your Son. Please watch over my family while I'm away and guide me on my journey. Bless the food to nourish my body. In Jesus' Name, Amen."

The plate was filled with an enchilada and all the accompanying fixings. Beside it, there a salad bowl accompanied several containers of dressing, a can of Sprite, a can of Dr. Pepper, and a cup of ice. A massive slice of pie completed the meal.

She opened the can of Dr. Pepper and poured it over the ice before taking a large forkful of the enchilada. Under different circumstances, she would have taken the time to savor the meal.

But now was not the time.

After finishing the meal, she stomped to the window and raised it. Only to find a steep drop kept her from considering jumping.

She lowered the window and went into the bathroom. A massive, tiled shower enclosed in glass drew Sylvia's eyes. Directly beside the shower sat a curved tub large enough for a swim.

The window above it would've fit in at a church from the old days. The thick glass design held a red heart in the middle, with shades of teal and pink blocks layered around the heart.

She gaped at the stark white and teal vanity with two teal sinks perched on the countertop.

But the strangest thing wasn't the bathroom. It was what was in the bathroom.

She opened the vanity drawer and slapped her hand across her mouth. It looked like the contents from her bathroom drawer had been transferred to this drawer. Her moisturizers and everything from her nightly routine sat nestled in the drawer.

But how?

Who could've known to bring all this stuff here?

Sylvia closed her eyes as heat traveled from her head to the soles of her feet. This wasn't a random kidnapping or misunderstanding. It was meticulous. Planned out down to even the littlest detail.

She had been the target.

Antonio Morales pointed at the door Sylvia banged on and lowered his voice. "See what I'm talking about?"

Louise shook her head. "Yes, Mr. Morales. I see your Evangeline is so confused."

"Thanks to your son, all will be well now that she's back home." Antonio's eyes glistened. "I just know it."

"Yes, sir. I believe she will be fine." The tension in Louise's stomach eased with the sincerity coming from Antonio. "Manuel was proud to help you find her and bring her home."

The door farthest down the hall clicked open, and Manuel Estrada strutted through the door. His black jeans and matching t-shirt played up the hint of danger emanating from him.

"You'll be well rewarded, Louise." He nodded in Manuel's direction. "You and your family."

Louise clapped her hands together. "Thank you, Mr. Morales. My Nicholas will die if Angel stays in prison. He must have a kidney, and I'm very grateful for your help."

"He'll be out very soon, and both your husband and son will be fine. I promise." He motioned for Louise to follow him down the hallway. "You and Manuel, keep my Evangeline taken care of."

Nicholas Estrada and Antonio had been neighbors and friends growing up. Even though Nicholas hadn't gotten personally involved in Antonio's Organized Crime Unit, he knew the Morales family were human labor traffickers.

Louise swallowed, trying her best to push those thoughts out of her mind. "I promise we'll take good care of your daughter."

# Chapter 9

"Knock knock!" Alvin said as he made his way up the steps of their deck, his muscles stretching against his white t-shirt.

Keatyn craned her neck past Alvin, her expression turning mischievous. "Where's the date?"

"Oh, she's coming. She got a phone call from her boss right when I got out." Alvin stared pointedly at Keatyn. "I came to remind you to be on your best behavior."

Keatyn let out a humph. "I'll be nice. Even though she's not Sylvia."

Strong waves crashed into the shore of Pensacola Beach. Alvin could lose himself in those waves. Instead, he let out a long, deep breath and shrugged. "That's not my fault. I've asked Sylvia out multiple times over the past two years, and she won't give me a chance. Maybe it's time to move on."

Gareth took the spot by Keatyn. "I say good for you. You've been pining over Sylvia for far too long."

Keatyn gripped Alvin's wrist. "But you love her. I know you do."

"Sometimes love isn't enough. At least when it's one-sided."

The conversation ended when Alvin's date walked up the stairs.

Keatyn's eyes got big when she came into sight.

Brinley Miller was not your average blonde. Though she was taller than most women, her body language could put even the meanest sailor at ease. She wore a flowing red top, black capris, and matching black wedges.

Alvin's lips lifted, "Family, this is Brinley Miller. Brinley, this is the fam."

Keatyn walked toward Brinley with her hand out. "Hi, Brinley, I'm Keatyn. This is my husband, Gareth, and our daughter, Lily."

"Hi, Keatyn and family." Brinley leaned down to Lily's level. "I love your sparkly flip-flops."

Lily followed Brinley's gaze and rubbed the black sparkles lining the top of the flip-flops. She grinned at Brinley. "Mommy got them for me!"

She returned Lily's smile as she stood and linked her arm to Alvin's. "Well, your mommy has great taste."

"She sure does." Gareth put his hand out to Brinley. "It's nice to meet you, Brinley."

"You, too," Brinley replied as she grasped Gareth's hand.

Keatyn raised her left brow, and Alvin's face lit up as if trying to convey that he knew Keatyn would like Brinley.

Removing his arm from Brinley's, Alvin ogled the food on the table. "I hope you made something good because I'm famished."

Keatyn shrugged, "Gareth did most of the cooking."

Alvin wiped his brow. "That's a relief."

"Ha ha ha, you've got jokes, I see," Keatyn smirked.

Alvin turned a blank expression on Keatyn and laid his right hand over his heart. "Who's joking?"

Keatyn went to elbow Alvin, but he side-stepped out of her reach. "You better hush before you run your date off."

Brinley gave out a half-laugh and settled her gaze on Alvin. "It'll take more than that to run me off, that's for sure."

Keatyn half smiled as she pulled a chair out. "Shall we sit?"

Gareth led a prayer of thanks after they made their plates.

Brinley lifted a fork full of vegetables and paused before reaching her mouth. "Alvin didn't know what he was talking about. This is delicious." Her eyes traveled across the white sand and blue waves. "And this view can't be beaten."

"Thanks," Keatyn replied. "This is certainly the best place to have dinner."

Gareth set his half-full glass of lemonade on the table. "So, Brinley, where do you attend service?"

Brinley used a knife to cut the corn off the cob. "Breakwater."

"Breakwater? Nice." Gareth shoveled in a hunk of medium-rare steak. "I heard Don Jones is retiring."

Brinley crossed her legs. "Sadly, yes."

"Have you been a member there long?" Gareth continued his line of questions.

Her head bobbed a quick nod. "Since I was a kid."

"That's great." Keatyn grinned. Alvin figured Brinley was looking better and better.

Keatyn's phone chimed from inside the house. She let it go to voicemail, and it immediately rang again.

Keatyn stood up from the chair. "I should check to see if everything is alright.

"Within minutes, Keatyn returned to the dinner party with sagging shoulders and a haunted expression.

Gareth's chair screeched across the patio as he abruptly stood up. "What's happened? Who was on the phone?"

Keatyn's voice came out so low they could barely hear what she said. "It was Sylvia's mom."

Alarm bells shot through Alvin. "What happened?"

Keatyn's fingers tightened around the table's smooth surface as she leaned forward, her brow furrowed with concern. "Sylvia is missing."

# Chapter 10

Alvin rang the doorbell at the Engle's residence and stepped back. He glanced at Keatyn and Gareth. "Thank you both for coming with me."

"No thanks needed. We love Sylvia, too." Keatyn said right before Jane Engle opened the door.

"Come on in, and please have a seat."

They followed her into the living area and took seats on the sofa. "Mrs. Jane, I don't know what's going on, but we've been praying so hard," Alvin said.

Jane met Keatyn's gaze. "Thank you, Alvin."

Gareth grasped Edgar's forearm. "What can we do for you both?"

Edgar sighed. "Praying is good. Jane's sister will be here soon to stay with the boys so we can join the search party."

"Dad and Cordelia are watching Lily so that Gareth can join in the search while I help prepare food for the volunteers. We wanted to bring some food by from our ladies."

"That's very kind. Please tell them we're grateful." Jane's voice caught on the last word.

Keatyn scooted closer to Jane and wrapped her arms around her neck. "I'm so sorry you're going through this. We'll do everything we can to find her."

"Everything." Alvin echoed. "We will continue in prayer, and we will search."

"That means so much to us both," Edgar replied.

Gareth leaned towards Jane and patted her knee. "I'd like to say a prayer before we leave."

Jane's eyes widened, and she glanced at Edgar. He nodded his head, and Jane met Gareth's dark gaze. "We would appreciate that very much."

# Chapter 11

Three long days had dragged by, with Sylvia only seeing Louise. A restless energy buzzed within her, making her heart race and palms sweat. Today marked the moment she had both dreaded and anticipated. Louise said she would finally come face to face with her captor.

"Miss Evangeline, it's time to get ready for dinner." Louise entered the closet and returned with Sylvia's cream-colored dress and strappy sandals.

Sylvia narrowed her eyes. "I don't need to wear that to dinner." She shrugged, pointing at her sporty black Nike sweatsuit, "I can wear what I have on."

"Oh, no, you most certainly will not." Louise clicked her tongue. "You know your father is a formal man and insists everyone at his table dresses the part for dinner. You'll wear the dress I selected."

Sylvia would've laughed if the situation hadn't been so serious. "My father is not formal and would never ask me to wear a dress to dinner."

Louise put a meaty hand on her hip. "I won't hear this nonsense. Get dressed, or I'll be forced to help you."

She managed a half smile, half grimace as she tugged her curly locks into a messy bun. "Fine. I guess it's good I get to meet my captor."

Louise shook her head. "You better get your attitude right before you meet your father."

"My attitude is as right as it's gonna get," Sylvia mumbled.

Louise sighed. "I'll be back in thirty minutes. Please be ready. And do something with your hair."

True to her word, Louise showed up precisely thirty minutes later. She nodded approval of Sylvia's dress, and her hair looked presentable in a tighter bun.

They walked down the hall and onto a grand staircase before entering the dining room. Gold and white curtains decorated two large windows, and a table in the center of the room was large enough to seat at least twenty people.

A woman dressed in a maid's uniform and a man in a suit stood against the wall. Sylvia furrowed her brows in confusion. The last time a butler had served her was at the Governor's Mansion, where she had attended a fundraiser for work.

The butler moved quickly to pull out a chair next to the head of the table. He nodded his head at the seat and smiled at Sylvia.

He spoke when Sylvia didn't move fast enough. "Madam, please be seated. Mr. Morales will join you momentarily."

Sylvia suddenly turned her head. "Mr. Morales?"

He ignored her.

It seemed like everyone around her lived in a dream world. They walked by as if she hadn't been assaulted and kidnapped. She wanted to ask one of them for help, but it looked like they were all part of it based on their demeanor.

Who would dare to kidnap the Prosecuting Attorney and keep her at their home? Her mind swirled with possibilities until she came face to face with the person behind it all.

Sylvia's mouth dropped open when Antonio Morales entered the room and sat at the head of the table. This was the same man for whom she had fought so hard for justice after the tragic loss of his daughter. During the trial, he'd worn his hair parted to the side and dressed in light gray or brown suits, looking like any typical businessman.

However, his jet-black hair was slicked back today, and he wore black dress pants and a silver button-up shirt. No one would mistake him for a typical businessman today. He reminded Sylvia of an actor from one of the old gangster movies.

"Why are you doing this?"

He held a slim finger up. "Please, no questions until after dinner, Evangeline."

Unable to stop herself, Sylvia's nostrils flared, and she slapped the table, nearly knocking over a glass of water. "Don't call me that. My name is Sylvia, and you know it."

With trembling hands, the maid placed a plate and bowl before Sylvia. Sylvia glanced at the woman, but she quickly averted her gaze.

Another woman in a matching outfit placed a dish in front of Antonio. He leaned close to his plate and took a sniff. Closing his eyes, he sighed with contentment. "This smells scrumptious."

Heat traveled up Sylvia's body, and she fought the urge to stab him with her butter knife. "I don't have an appetite."

Antonio's eyes widened. "But it is Pulled Pork Tamales, Corn Salsa, and a Salad. Your favorite dishes. You must eat, my dear."

Sylvia studied his eyes intently, noticing the wildness in them that hinted at his unraveling mind. She knew all too well that those who had lost their grip on reality could be the most dangerous. A chill ran down her spine as she weighed her options, acutely aware that she was treading on thin ice. Her instincts screamed for her to back off and avoid pushing him further.

With a reluctant sigh, she relented, her voice steady yet cautious. "Fine."

Antonio gripped Sylvia's hand. "You've made me so happy. Now, let us say a prayer of thanks for the food."

Her prison ward wanted to pray. That's priceless.

Afterward, he took a bite of the Tamale and shook his head up and down. He continued to stare at Sylvia until she took her first bite. After Sylvia swallowed the bite of food, his lips stretched wide, and he turned his attention back to his plate.

After a few minutes, Sylvia caught him staring at her. "Why are you looking at me like that?"

The edge of his mouth lifted as he dabbed it with a white napkin. "It's happiness causing me to look as I do. You're here with me, and you're safe. This is now my number one priority. You'll never be allowed to leave this place again."

# Chapter 12

Jane clutched Ed's arm as they walked up the steps at the side of the Fort Hill church of Christ. "Ed, I don't know if I can do it."

Ed covered Jane's hand in his. "Honey, this is for Sylvia. Remember, we didn't get ostracized by the people here."

Jane looked down at her white sandals, "I know. It feels weird going into a church building after so many years."

He squeezed her hand and kissed the top of her head. "Everything will be fine. I promise."

Jane's sister, Martha, piped in. "I agree with Edgar. The police will find Sylvia safe and sound. And having people praying for her will help so much."

Looking at them, you wouldn't know they were sisters. Jane was tall and slender, and Martha was shorter and stockier.

Despair attacked Jane's insides. "You think this will help our baby girl be found?"

"There's power in prayer. Like Martha, I do believe that." Edgar replied.

Jane screwed up her lips and tilted her head. "You do? Why have you never said anything?"

Ed pressed his lips together. "I honestly don't have the answer to your question. Tell you what, let's go in here and support Gareth as he and their members pray. We can talk about the rest later."

"All right." Jane's features softened. "For Sylvia."

Keatyn pulled the door open. "I'm so glad y'all are here."

Jane moved through the door ahead of Ed and Martha and hugged Keatyn. "Thank you for doing this." She pointed at Martha. "This is my sister Martha Williams."

"Hello, Martha." Keatyn shook her hand. "Please help yourselves to something to eat and drink."

"Thank you," Martha replied.

"Where are the boys?"

"We talked to the school, and they're allowing the boys to leave school a few days early. Martha will take the boys home with her for a while. We don't want them seeing anything on the local news." Edgar commented.

Keatyn bobbed her head. "That's a good plan."

They walked into the kitchen, and several church members greeted them.

Kyle VanHouten and his two-year-old daughter, Bliss, joined them. He put his free hand out, and

Ed and Jane shook it, followed by Martha. "I'm Kyle VanHouten, and this is Bliss." He pointed to his wife, who was busy setting the food out. "That's my wife, Rebecca."

After exchanging a greeting, Jane noticed several women buzzing around, setting food trays on the counter. "So, what's going on?"

"We've turned the kitchen area into a base for the volunteers. They can come here to freshen up and eat before rejoining the search." Gareth explained as he approached.

Myles and Cordelia Griffin walked through the doors, with Lily trailing behind them. Myles carried two platters of sandwiches, while Cordelia and Lily each had bags of chips.

Cordelia set the chips on the counter and walked straight to Jane with her arms outstretched.

Jane's eyes got big, but she stepped into Cordelia's embrace. "You must be Jane. I can't even imagine what you're going through. We've been praying nonstop for Sylvia's safe return."

Jane's voice shook when she spoke. "That means so much."

Myles shook Edgar's hand. "Please let us know if we can do anything for y'all. Anything at all. I'm Myles Griffin, and this is my wife, Cordelia."

Edgar grasped Myles' hand. "You have all done so much already. We can't begin to thank you."

Martha smiled. "I wish we were here under better conditions. I'm Jane's sister, Martha Williams."

"Yes, ma'am. We'll have to plan a get-together once Sylvia is home." Cordelia responded.

Jane's eyes softened. "I'd like that."

Alvin and one of his friends walked inside a little later, followed by two policemen.

Keatyn marched up to Alvin. "Any updates?"

Molly Johnson, one of the single volunteers, whisked the police officers over to the refreshment table.

Alvin raised a brow but kept his attention on Keatyn. "The police have sectioned off our search areas. We've ruled out many of Pensacola's trails and wooded areas."

"I guess that's something, at least." Keatyn glanced at Alex Foster, Alvin's friend. "Hi, Alex. Thank you so much for helping."

Alex's lips lifted slightly at the corners, causing his green eyes to sparkle against his fiery red hair. "I wouldn't be able to live with myself if I wasn't helping in the search." Daniel Bradford waved Alex over, and he touched Keatyn's forearm. "Excuse me, looks like Daniel needs to speak to me."

Alvin looked around. "Where are the boys?"

Martha piped in. "With my daughter, Lisa. I'm Jane's sister, Martha."

Alvin introduced himself before continuing, "Do they know?"

"No, we decided to wait a few more days before telling them." Edgar paused as a few more people entered the kitchen. "If we tell them at all."

Alvin turned to ask the police officers to join him for lunch, and a half-smile crossed his mouth. They had their plates and were already at a table, with Molly Johnson sitting directly between them.

# Chapter 13

Sylvia threw her leg out from underneath the cover and stared at the ceiling. She rolled over. She thought about her boys, and a heaviness covered her chest.

She rose from the bed and walked to the bathroom, quickly rinsing her face. There had to be a reason she was here. The sermon Gareth preached the Sunday before had been about turning trials into triumphs. Maybe she could figure out how to turn the nightmare she found herself in into a triumph.

She racked her brain, trying to remember the Bible verse that stuck with her, and after a few minutes, it hit her.

She hightailed it back to the bedroom and pulled the nightstand drawer out. Sure enough, her Bible lay in the drawer.

She read Romans 5:3.

*"And not only so, but we glory in tribulations also:
knowing that tribulation worketh patience."*

She remembered Gareth saying to count it all joy when Satan attacks. He said having the right knowledge concerning the value of trials makes it possible for us to have a joyful attitude.

These things test our faith. Our faith, when tested, makes us stronger as we overcome, and these trials bring out the best in us and glorify God.

He preached that the key to turning trials into triumph is having the knowledge and perspective that adversity can accomplish much good.

We must allow adversity to accomplish its work within us. We can do this by using the wisdom God gives in answer to prayer, helping to put it all together. And when this is done, even trials can be a source of joy for the Christian,

We are blessed and privileged, and God has given us the key to turning trials into triumphs. She nodded her head. Time to figure out how to apply Gareth's sermon to her situation. There had to be a way.

A knock at the door snapped Sylvia out of her deep thought. "Come in."

Louise came in and stopped in her tracks, her eyes landing on the open Bible. "What are you doing?"

Sylvia shifted on the bed. "Studying and trying to figure out why I've been brought here."

"Oh?" Louise stared from Sylvia to the Bible. "And have you come to a conclusion?"

"I think I'm here for a reason." Sylvia blinked. "I believe God plans to use me to further His cause in a way I don't know about yet."

Louise dropped her eyes to the floor.

Sylvia recognized Louise's wheels turning. "What's on your mind?"

Louise stiffened, worry spreading across her brow. "Never mind. Get ready for a walk with your father."

""All right." Sylvia glanced at the ceiling, half expecting it to open for her escape. "Give me ten minutes."

Louise hurried out the door but paused before she closed it. "Make sure to bring an umbrella with you. There's a mist in the wind from the rain last night."

"I will. Thank you." A faint smile appeared. "I'm not Evangeline Morales. She tragically passed away in a car accident. My name is Sylvia Mason."

Louise's shoulders drooped, but she didn't respond as the door snapped shut behind her.

Sylvia gathered her rain jacket and umbrella before turning to Psalms 147:3-6.

*"He heals the brokenhearted And binds up their wounds. He counts the number of the stars; He calls them all by name. Great is our Lord, and mighty in power; His understanding is infinite. The Lord lifts up the humble; He casts the wicked down to the ground."*

As she finished the last verse, a knock broke the quiet. She looked at the delicate text, her fingers brushing the worn pages as she stepped away from the room, letting her thoughts guide her.

# Chapter 14

Antonio placed Sylvia's hand in the crook of his arm as they walked through the flower garden. Under different circumstances, she would've stopped to admire the Cherry Blossoms, pink roses, and white lilies that lined the garden's cobblestone path.

A stream flowing over medium-sized white boulders ran down the left side of the garden. Sylvia walked up a white curved bridge, the only way to reach the red and white roses surrounding a pink bench.

The view from the top of the bridge took Sylvia's breath away. Beyond the fence, a field of red flowers seemed to go on forever. The sun sat perfectly shrouded in golden yellow above the area, casting its rays on the red flowers.

After a few minutes, Antonio motioned for Sylvia to come down.

Stepping off the bridge, she glared at the tall, muscular man who followed a few feet behind her. He was the very man who had kidnapped her. His name was Manuel, and he had a connection to Louise, but she still hadn't figured out what it was.

Sylvia's forehead creased with worry, but she kept her hand on Antonio's arm. "Please tell me why you're doing this to me. I miss my family."

Antonio stopped in front of a rose bush. "Isn't this a beautiful bush? The scent calms my soul."

She frowned. "That's great, but you didn't answer me."

"Come, Evangeline, let us continue our walk in peace." He continued walking through the garden, tugging her along with him.

"My name is Sylvia." Her legs shook with the urge to stomp her feet and jump up and down.

He seemed oblivious. "Do you remember when you were ten and begged me to put a flower garden here?"

No, because I'm not Evangeline."

Antonio's eyes glazed over, like his mind was in a different time and place. "You were so cute. The way you put your hands on your hips and demanded you have the garden to remember your late mama. All because you loved a rose garden we saw while visiting your grandparents in Japan."

The wind carried the sound of horses neighing from the barn behind the house. Which gave Sylvia the idea of possibly escaping on horseback. At this point, she'd be willing to flee on a donkey.

How could he discuss events pertaining to his daughter as though Sylvia had experienced them herself? It felt like a regular day-to-day conversation. Did he not recognize that Sylvia was with him against her will? Had he forgotten that detail? No. Clearly, something else was happening.

Antonio continued, "You got your way, as always. I had Ricardo oversee the work, and you had your garden before long." He paused and cocked his head to the left. "Have you seen Ricardo lately?"

Sylvia shook her head.

"He'll be home soon, I'm sure. That boy is always up to something." Antonio covered Sylvia's hand in his own.

Sylvia kicked a rock lying in her path. "Is Ricardo married?"

Antonio closed his eyes. "Your sickness is further along than I thought. How do you not remember your brother?"

"I guess because he's not my brother." She emphasized the last four words.

"He's not married. Ricardo has never been one to settle down. You should know this." A sad look passed over his features.

"Okay. Where is he now?"

His shoulders slumped, and his eyes drifted to the sky. "He's on a trip. I do believe he is." He pointed at a wooden sign. "Do you at least remember naming your garden after your mama? You had to name it Rosalinda's Garden."

Sylvia met Antonio's eyes, and her stomach flipped. This man was genuinely sick.

Antonio patted her hand. "Your sister and her husband are here. You'll get to have your reunion at dinner."

A bit of hope flashed through Sylvia's bones. "Really?"

His eyes searched hers. "Yes, are you excited to see Kemena?"

"Very much so." Sylvia honestly replied.

A grin split Antonio's lip. "You remember your sister. This is good news."

# Chapter 15

Sylvia's mind raced as she walked down the stairs for dinner. She prayed that Kemena had enough sense to ensure Antonio received help for his delusions and to let Sylvia return home.

She entered the dining room on pins and needles. Antonio sat at the head of the table, while a couple faced away from Sylvia. A rush of tingling excitement coursed through Sylvia's body as she approached the table.

The man turned his head to speak to the butler as Sylvia made her way around the table.

Sylvia's gaze settled on the woman before anything else. She was clearly Antonio's daughter. Dark curls cascaded down her shoulders, and her feminine face displayed a mix of surprise and animosity. The white jumpsuit she wore provided a striking contrast to her olive skin.

"Who's this?" the woman Sylvia assumed to be Kemena asked Antonio.

Before Antonio could respond, the woman's husband rose so quickly that his chair tipped over. Sylvia startled at the noise and focused her attention on the man.

Soft blue eyes which had once looked at her with deep affection, now widened in disbelief as they bore into her. "Sylvia? What on earth are you doing here?" Lee Mason exclaimed, his voice a mix of confusion and concern.

Sylvia clutched the table, her nails scraping against the wood. "What am I doing here? What are you doing here? I thought you were dead!"

Antonio nodded, and Manuel moved closer to Sylvia, placing his hand on her shoulder.

Kemena wrapped her arm around Lee's waist. Her upper lip curled as she looked down her nose at Sylvia. "Sweetheart, who is this woman?" she asked.

Lee cast a worried glance at the woman. "Kemena, this is Sylvia."

Kemena raised her voice. "What? How?" Anger flashed in her eyes as she pressed her palm on her stomach and stared at Lee.

Sylvia's mouth dropped open, but she couldn't find the words. What could she possibly say?

Did people thrown into an episode of The Twilight Zone ever speak, or did they just stand around in stunned silence? She couldn't recall a single episode, even though she had watched them all.

"Hey," Lee whispered as he extended his arms towards Kemena.

Just as he reached her, Kemena's hand struck his cheek with a sharp crack. He raised his hands in defense, eyes wide with shock. "I had no idea my ex would be here," he exclaimed, desperation creeping in. Turning to Antonio, he searched for answers. "Why would you bring Sylvia here?"

Antonio tilted his head. "You mean Evangeline?"

"What madness are you raving about?" Kemena yelled.

Antonio chuckled but remained silent.

Lee rested his hand on Kemena's wrist. "I believe your father is confused."

"What have you done?" Kemena glared at Antonio. "If you weren't insane, you'd meet the same fate as Ricardo."

Antonio looked back at Kemena with emotionless black eyes. "I've done nothing."

Kemena's voice cut through the room like a cold blade, her tone sharp and uncaring. Sylvia felt the words scrape against her insides, a reminder of the pain she was trying to avoid. "You understand that Evangeline is gone, don't you?"

"I'm not the one who's confused." Antonio moved next to where Manuel held Sylvia. "You should show your sister more respect."

"That woman is not my sister." Kemena picked up a glass of water and threw it across the room, shattering it.

Anger surged in Sylvia's throat, and she lunged across the table, her eyes locked on Kemena.

Kemena stepped back from the table, and her bodyguard seized Sylvia before she could reach the other side. Her vision faded to white as her pulse throbbed in her ears.

Screams of denial clogged her throat as she fought to escape the bodyguard. The sting of his nails bit into her arms as she struggled to reach Kemena.

A sudden pinch in her neck caused Sylvia to go stock still. In the background, Antonio and Kemena argued as the bodyguard handed Sylvia off to Manuel.

The drug coursed through her system as Manuel carried her out of the room. Her arms dropped to her sides like anchors on a boat, heavy and difficult to move.

# Chapter 16

As Manuel carried Sylvia upstairs, she began to regain consciousness. As soon as Manuel laid her on the bed, she heard Louise's voice raised in anger.

"What are you doing here, Madre?"

"You had better tell me what's going on. And I mean now."

"Please don't ask this of me."

"I'm not asking."

"The woman will not be harmed. Mr. Morales promised me this."

"The woman? The one you and Mr. Morales have tried to trick me into believing is his dead daughter? Rest her soul."

"Yes."

"Yes? This is all you have to say for yourself?"

Sylvia cautiously opened her eyes just a slit, taking in her surroundings. She noticed Manuel sitting nearby, his face buried in his hands, a picture of distress.

"No, Madre," he said, a tinge of regret emanating from his voice. "I didn't see another way to save papa."

"So, you decided to do this horrible thing. Do you think your Papa would be proud of you?"

His voice was close to a whisper. "No, Madre."

"Are you the one who kidnapped this poor innocent woman?"

Manuel's eyes landed on the floor.

Louise balked. "This is my answer. You did this thing."

"I'm sorry." A worried expression crossed his face. "I wish I'd never agreed to come here. To bring you here. This is my fault."

Her brow puckered, and her tone was stern. "You will fix this."

He let out a huff. "How am I going to do that?"

"Think about it tonight and let me know tomorrow. You better have a plan to make things right."

"Yes, Madre." He replied.

Heat licked Sylvia's body, and her vision blurred with red splotches of fumes. She ignored the throbbing traveling from her hand and wrist to her arm and continued slamming her fist into the door.

She tried to recall the conversation between Louise and Manuel, but all she could remember were fragments.

The one thing she was certain of was that Louise had not been involved in her kidnapping.

Perhaps she could convince Louise to escape with her.

"Let me out of here!" Sylvia yelled until the air in her lungs evaporated.

A flicker of seething hatred sizzled its way through her chest, followed by a deep gurgling scream. "Lee! I thought you were dead!"

Flinging herself on the bed, she wailed into the pillow until the bedroom door clicked open. Antonio stood there with a sorrowful expression. "My dear, I'm so sorry you're hurting."

Jerking herself into a sitting position, dark eyes shot daggers at Antonio. "Sorry?" She stomped towards where he stood. "You're sorry? Liar!"

Antonio stepped out of the bedroom, quickly locking the door behind him.

Sylvia didn't bother trying to open the door. Instead, she attempted to push her feelings of hatred aside, but it was in vain.

She had mourned her husband deeply, to the point that she had pushed away a good man. At least now she knew that was for the best, considering she was still a married woman.

That line of thought wasn't helping. So, she tried to look on the bright side. Lee was alive. But with another woman.

Her eyes fell on her wedding ring. Springing to her feet, she slammed the bathroom door open. Stopping in front of the toilet, she stared at the ring, twisting it around her finger as she had done for the past five years.

Her mind flashed back to her wedding day, recalling the gleam in Lee's eyes as she stood beside him, vowing to love him until death do them part. He stood next to her, promising the same.

She remembered how Lee had held her close, shared his hopes and dreams for their future, and expressed his love for her with just a simple look.

She yanked the ring off her finger and dropped it into the toilet. As the water swirled, the ring settled onto the white porcelain.

She flushed the toilet and walked away, leaving not just the ring behind but also Lee.

After an hour of intense anger, a deep sadness caused nausea to permeate her body.

She kept asking herself why Lee had done this to her.

Was this betrayal planned?

What mistakes had she made that led to this moment?

Did she not measure up?

Was the trouble in their lives a sign of her own failures?

As this heartbreak overwhelmed her, she realized that Lee's actions had not only hurt her but also their boys, leaving her feeling lost in the chaos.

Thinking about the boys turned her despair back to anger. She'd shoot Lee if she could get her hands on a gun.

Sylvia's heart raced at the thought.

Her mind was so troubled that she let negativity creep in.

It felt as if blisters were bursting inside her.

Yes, Lee had treated her horribly, but how much worse was what happened to Christ?

He came to save us and was subjected to unimaginable suffering.

Did He think of hurting those who hurt Him?

Absolutely not. Instead, He prayed for them.

She bowed her head and prayed aloud.

"Dear Heavenly Father, thank You for life, family, and Your Son. Please comfort my family and keep them safe while I'm away."

She paused to blow her nose before continuing her prayer.

"Father, I pray that You will be with me during this situation that I don't understand. Help me to accept it and to do my best to bring honor and glory to Your Name. I pray for Mr. Morales, that he may find comfort in the loss of his daughter and that his mind may be eased. I also pray for Lee, that Your will is done."

Tears ran down her face as she finished.

When he looked up, she met Louise's sad gaze.

Louise slowly walked to the bed and leaned to eye level with Sylvia. "My son and I have wronged you, and I'm sorry." Her voice broke. "I'll do what I can to make this right."

Louise dashed out of the room before Sylvia had a chance to reply.

# Chapter 17

Alvin bowed his head and prayed for Sylvia's safe return as hot water streamed over his scalp. A few minutes later, he began scrubbing his hair with Pantene shampoo.

He had just over an hour before his Navy buddy Darren would arrive, and together they would continue the search for Sylvia.

They planned a trip to Blackwater to search for anything unusual. Even though he felt like he might be grasping at straws, he couldn't just sit around doing nothing—not while waiting for Sylvia to come home.

As the hot water dripped down his hair and face, he continued to pray. He held onto the hope that Sylvia would return safely. His faith wouldn't allow him to consider any other possibility.

Half an hour later, as the rich aroma of freshly brewed coffee filled the kitchen, Alvin found himself pouring another steaming cup when the sharp ring of the doorbell cut through his thoughts.

With a quick glance at the clock, he set the coffee pot down and pulled on a well-worn gray Navy t-shirt, its fabric soft and familiar against his skin. He jogged to the door.

Brinley had nearly reached her car when he cleared his throat. She turned around, her hand flying to her throat. "Oh, hi," she said, her voice shaking.

He raised his eyebrows. "What's going on? Is everything okay?"

Brinley glanced toward Keatyn's beach house. "I need to talk to you," she said.

Alvin stepped outside and waved for Brinley to join him on the front porch swing. "What's up?" he asked.

Brinley swallowed hard and glanced at her watch. "Listen, I don't want to add any more pressure, but I don't think things are working out between us."

At that moment, Alvin's neighbor backed out of his driveway, and a ray of early morning sunshine hit Alvin directly in the eyes. He raised his hand as a shield and squinted at Brinley. "Really? Why not?"

Brinley bit her bottom lip. "It's just not ideal right now."

Alvin shrugged and tilted his head thoughtfully, a hint of confusion in his eyes. "I know we've only been on a few dates, but I genuinely thought you were interested in pursuing a relationship with me."

Brinley glanced down for a moment, pulling her jacket tighter around herself as if seeking comfort from a chill. "I was, but I've noticed you've already given your heart to someone else," she replied, her voice tinged with disappointment.

His chin lifted a degree. "That's news to me. Who do you think I'm already taken by?" He patted the seat. "Sit down so we can talk this through."

She parked herself next to Alvin and rubbed the back of her neck. "You know who. And as soon as she comes home, the two of you can be together."

A sigh escaped his lips. "Are you talking about Sylvia?"

Brinley's face reddened, and she looked away. "Yes, I am. Please don't deny you have feelings for her."

Alvin hung his head, and a half-smile littered with disappointment crossed his face. "Are you mad because I'm spending time searching for Sylvia?"

"What? Of course not." Brinley's eyebrows pulled together. "That has nothing to do with this."

Alvin inwardly winced. "All right, I'm sorry. I shouldn't have said that."

"It's okay." Her mouth turned down. "I've known you had feelings for Sylvia for a while, but I was hoping I could help you get over her."

For a moment, Alvin considered denying Brinley's claim, but he realized that it would be a lie.

Instead, he pressed his lips together and looked into her concerned gaze. "Honestly, Brinley, I was hoping for the same thing. Please forgive me for not being honest with you when I asked you out."

Brinley shook her finger. "It's okay. We weren't engaged or in a serious relationship. I understand." Alvin let out the breath he had been holding. "Thank you for saying what I couldn't."

Brinley held her hand out. "Still friends?"

Alvin shook her hand. "Absolutely."

A blue Jeep Wrangler 4x4 pulled into the drive, and Darren Bartlett hopped out of the driver's seat. His tan skin glistened against his white Navy t-shirt and brown utility shorts. "Morning."

Alvin pulled himself out of the swing set and grasped Darren's forearm in a man-hug. "Morning, I can't tell you how much I appreciate you helping with the search."

Darren took off his ballcap, revealing black curls cut close to his head. "Nothing could have stopped me." He nodded in Brinley's direction. "Is this the girlfriend?"

"No, no, I'm not." Brinley stepped in front of Alvin and stuck her hand out. "Brinley Miller, nice to meet you."

"The pleasure is all mine," Darren replied as he wrapped her hand in his.

"She's definitely single."  Alvin looked back and forth from Brinley to Darren and raised his left eyebrow a notch before muttering under his breath, "For now, at least."

# Chapter 18

Seeking clarity amid her tumultuous emotions, Sylvia stepped into the vibrant spring garden, clutching her cherished Bible. Surrounded by colorful blooms and sweet fragrances, she pondered how a woman could reconcile the deep ache of betrayal that had shattered her world.

She opened her Bible to 1 Peter 5:10 and read the verse several times.

*"But may the God of all grace, who called us to His eternal glory by Christ Jesus, after you have suffered a while, perfect, establish, strengthen, and settle you."*

She read the verse aloud, then looked up just in time to see a thick cloud slide over the sun, creating a halo effect. An emptiness that she thought about embracing crept into her bones, and a flicker of hatred ignited in her heart. Her mind wandered to Lee, and she envisioned him moving on effortlessly, as if she had never been part of his life. A bitter laugh escaped her lips, laced with disbelief and resentment. Could he truly forget her so easily? Determined to push those feelings aside, she returned to reading the Bible.

Turning to chapter 138 of the Psalms, she read a passage she had highlighted earlier. She paused at verse 7 and reread it several times.

*"Though I walk in the midst of trouble, You will revive me; You will stretch out Your hand against the wrath of my enemies, and Your right hand will save me."*

As the scent of roses drifted through the air, Sylvia closed her eyes, trying to forget that her husband had left her for another woman.

It was pointless. She couldn't ignore it or pretend it hadn't happened.

This was the real world, and she had a choice to either let Lee drive her to despair or trust in God to help her through.

King David faced many trials in his life, and the Bible described him as a man after God's heart. Even after experiencing loss and betrayal, he remained committed to seeking God.

How could she be more like David?

Thinking back to the last class Alvin taught, Sylvia flipped over to the book of 2 Samuel, scanning the pages until she reached chapter 22.

She smiled as she read verses 1 through 7, recalling how nervous Alvin had been to teach. He never would've imagined those verses would be just what Sylvia would need.

*"Then David spoke to the Lord the words of this song, on the day when the Lord had delivered him from the hand of all his enemies, and from the hand of Saul. And he said: "The Lord is my rock and my fortress and my deliverer; The God of my strength, in whom I will trust; My shield and the horn of my salvation, My stronghold and my refuge; My Savior, You save me from violence. I will call upon the Lord, who is worthy to be praised; So shall I be saved from my enemies. "When the waves of death surrounded me, The floods of ungodliness made me afraid. The sorrows of Sheol surrounded me; The snares of death confronted me. In my distress I called upon the Lord, And cried out to my God; He heard my voice from His temple, And my cry entered His ears."*

Staring out into the field, Sylvia reflected on what Alvin had said. "Jehovah God represents a rock like a solid foundation for man to stand upon. Do y'all know God will never fail the faithful? He is a refuge when we face hard times or storms in our lives. We should call out to God in times of distress."

The sound of heavy footsteps reverberated off the wooden planks of the bridge, prompting Sylvia to glance over her shoulder.

Kemena sauntered towards her, a smirk on her face.

A shiver raced down Sylvia's spine, igniting a chilling sensation that contrasted sharply with the warmth around her.

"Well, if it isn't the fake wife," Kemena spat venomously as she crossed the bridge.

Sylvia ignored the comments and continued reading the Bible verses.

Kemena stopped in front of Sylvia, kicking the Bible out of her hands. The Bible landed in the stream.

Sylvia scampered to her feet and scooped the Bible out of the water.

Before she could think twice, Sylvia lunged forward with a sudden surge of anger, her fists clenched tight. She aimed a hard punch at Kemena's face, the force of her blow sending Kemena sprawling to the ground, stunned and wide-eyed.

The air crackled with tension as Sylvia stood over her, adrenaline coursing through her veins.

Apparently, not one to take a beating, Kemena grabbed Sylvia's long hair, slinging her to the ground. Shoving her arm into Sylvia's throat, she pressed with all her might.

Sylvia flailed her arms until Kemena pressed a blade to her throat. "Do not move, or I'll cut your throat."

A droplet of blood fell onto Sylvia's cheek from Kemena's bloody nose, and Sylvia regretted her actions. "Please forgive me for attacking you," she gasped, struggling for breath.

Ignoring Sylvia, Kemena shouted, "Oliver! Get over here, now!"

Oliver, Kemena's bodyguard, bolted over the bridge and gasped. "I'm sorry, boss"

"Shut up and bring this trash to the barn," Kemena said, emphasizing the word trash. "It's time she's taught a lesson on respect."

# Chapter 19

W hen Sylvia was a teenager, she accidentally dropped a pan of boiling water into the sink. Some of the water splashed onto her arm, causing her intense pain. She cried until the doctor gave her a cream that provided tremendous relief.

Now, after just ten minutes with Oliver strapping her back, Sylvia would welcome that pot of boiling water any day.

A gunshot echoed inside the barn.

Oliver fell to the ground with a thud.

Someone untied Sylvia, picked her up, and rushed out of the barn.

Sylvia's eyes rolled back in her head as she took a shallow breath. Fiery, intense spasms coursed down her back, stopping at her waistline.

A little later, Sylvia opened her eyes, struggling to recall how she ended up on her stomach in a moving vehicle.

She tried to roll onto her back, but her body collapsed. A cool sensation replaced the burning hot spasms, and she sighed.

"Please be still," a kind voice she recognized as Louise's said from above.

"Did Kemena have me whipped?" Sylvia turned her head to look at Louise.

"Yes, that devil, Kemena, had you horse-whipped." Louise's forehead creased, and a slice of anger laced her words. She leaned close to Sylvia's ear. "Thankfully, my Manuel ran and got Mr. Morales, and he was able to stop it before she hurt you too badly."

Sylvia would have to disagree with that notion.

She cracked her eyes open, and the dim light allowed her to make out a small kitchenette. "Where are we?"

"In a van that Mr. Morales owns. Heading some-place safe."

Sylvia's mind raced. "Why?"

"Mr. Morales felt it best if we left. He has been on the phone finding a safe place for us to go." Louise handed Sylvia a small pill and a water. "Here, take this muscle relaxer."

Turning her head to the side, Sylvia moaned. "I don't want to take a pill."

"Please." Louise patted Sylvia's hand. "It's to help ease your pain."

"I guess you could've already killed me if that was the plan," Sylvia said as she inspected the pill. Did she say that out loud?

Louise clicked her tongue. "No one is going to kill you."

Sylvia obliged, swishing the water and pill in her mouth before swallowing. "I want to go home."

Louise held onto a bar as the van swerved. "In due time, I promise I'll help you get home."

"You promise?" Sylvia couldn't keep the sliver of hope out of her voice.

Louise turned Sylvia's face by her chin until their eyes met. "I give you my word. I'll see you get home safe and sound, Miss Sylvia."

The muscle relaxer kicked in a few minutes later, and Sylvia surrendered her mind to sleep.

"We have arrived at our destination." Louise patted Sylvia's arm. "Take care not to move too quickly."

"You don't have to worry about that. Believe me," Sylvia grunted.

In a matter of minutes, Manuel and another man assisted Sylvia out of the van and through a set of large mahogany double doors leading into a Caribbean-style home.

As the door closed behind her, she lightly ran her hand down the glass on the inside.

The house's exterior was lovely, but the interior left Sylvia speechless. Deep brown polished wooden floors connected the living area to the kitchen, while a white fireplace was centrally located among expansive windows.

Manuel sat down at the kitchen table while the other guard went out the front door. Sylvia looked around and attempted to get up, but a surge of pain shot down her back, forcing her to lower herself back down.

Bowing her head, Sylvia asked God to forgive her for her involvement in the altercation. After praying, she continued scanning her surroundings, devising a plan to escape.

# Chapter 20

Violet rays streamed through the window, casting an ethereal glow on the white bedding in Sylvia's latest jail cell bedroom. She rubbed her hands down her arms and squinted at the wooded area beyond the balcony, trying to identify the best escape route.

She wasn't naïve; she understood that escaping into the woods could be dangerous. But what choice did she have?

With her back pain nearly gone, she could no longer wait for rescue. Loneliness filled her heart as memories of her boys flooded her mind. She longed to embrace them again and feel their warmth and joy.

Although her heart ached for Antonio, she had to prioritize her family. He needed serious therapy, and she was no therapist.

Finding Lee was like a wound to her heart. He made Sylvia and their boys believe he was dead, leaving them for another woman and a life of crime.

She had once planned to build a life with him. She had loved him and remained faithful even after thinking he had died. Now, all she felt was pity for the man who had lived a lie for over two years. She loved his soul, but that was all.

A soft knock interrupted her thoughts. When she opened the door, Antonio stood there, looking contrite. Sylvia left the door open and sat down, gazing out the window.

Antonio tiptoed over and sat down across from her. "I can't express how sorry I am for what your sister did to you back there. I promise I will never let anything like that happen to you again. The police have taken her into custody."

"What about Lee?"

Tenting his long fingers, he cleared his throat before answering. "He's in the wind. No telling where he is, but I don't think he'll try to hurt you, Evangeline."

She met his remorseful eyes with a fiery gaze. "You have no idea, do you? Or are you trying to play me for a fool like Lee did?"

His shoulders drooped, and he closed his eyes. "I see you're still upset with me."

"Upset?" Sylvia answered, stuffing her balled-up fists underneath her legs.

"Yes, I understand why you're upset." He stood quickly. "But don't worry, my dear. I'll make sure you never see Kemena again. We'll leave at dawn."

Sylvia swallowed the lump in her throat and stared at him, dumbfounded.

Antonio placed both hands on Sylvia's shoulders. "I see you're so pleased that it's left you speechless. Good."

She cut her eyes to meet Antonio's. "Leaving to go where?"

"Venezuela." With that, Antonio kissed her forehead and disappeared through the bedroom door.

<h1 style="text-align:center">Chapter 21</h1>

The pond outside Sylvia's window lit white briefly as a flash of lightning traveled in the distance above Perdido Key Beach. Sylvia prayed the storm would stay above the sea and not venture too close to where she was.

A storm would be inconvenient and could possibly hinder her escape. And there was no way she would be going to Venezuela.

No way.

They'd have to drag her dead body because she would not be going as long as she had breath.

It was almost two in the morning. She planned to make a run for it at two on the dot.

Using a bobby pin as her means of escape.

She'd been ecstatic when she found one in the corner of the bathroom drawer earlier that day.

And it just so happened that she was an expert at picking locks using bobby pins. Thanks to Oakland.

He had a bad habit of locking himself in the bathroom, so Sylvia had used a bobby pin to unlock the door more than once.

She glanced into her getaway bag and felt satisfied with its contents: three bottles of water, a can of Sprite, two muffins, some Oreos, and three crackers.

She hoped to find help before the food ran out.

The doorknob clicked, causing Sylvia to freeze in place. Shivers passed from her throat to her stomach as she stood still, waiting for someone to enter the room.

Her eyes remained pinned to the door. She pulled the butcher knife she'd taken from the kitchen the night before out from underneath her mattress.

Seconds passed without anyone entering the room. Sylvia strung the satchel across her shoulders and pulled on a pair of thick socks while keeping the knife by her side.

Knife in hand, Sylvia swallowed and padded to the door. Her fingers wrapped around the doorknob, and she breathed in a steadying breath.

Preparing to use the bobby pin, she let out an almost silent gasp when she found the door unlocked.

Knowing it could be a trap only caused a moment's hesitation. She had to get out of there. This very night or she may never see the boys again.

All because a madman wanted her to be the daughter he lost.

The door swung open without a peep. Scanning the hallway, she found it empty. Thankful to the Lord, she eased out of the bedroom.

Even though silence met her, goosebumps pimpled down her arms and legs. She took several faltering steps before pausing at the top of the stairs.

The rooms below held nothing but darkness and shadows. At least as far as Sylvia could tell. There could be someone lurking, waiting to drag her back to her prison. Determined to stop worrying about what could be, she continued moving as quietly as possible.

The air in her lungs seemed to evaporate as she crept down the stairs. But nothing would deter her. She had a mission. Get out and get home.

Setting her sights on the front door, she picked up her pace as quickly and quietly as possible. As soon as her feet landed on the bottom step, she took off at breakneck speed, which could've landed her the winner of any race.

# Chapter 22

Despite the warm night air, Sylvia's teeth chattered as she ran deeper into the woods behind the house. Determined, she pushed herself to go faster.

Lightning flashed across the sky, creating a vivid purple display.

After a few minutes, she found a pathway that felt strangely familiar. Maybe home was closer than she realized!

A rumbling bellow echoed from her right as she stepped onto the wooden path.  Sylvia's spine jolted at the sound, and she ran her hand along the rail, hoping it was sturdy enough to keep unwanted visitors from joining her on the path. Unfortunately, it wasn't.

Another rumble brought back memories of the motorcycle her high school boyfriend used to ride.

What made that sound? She'd heard it before, but couldn't place where.

She racked her brain until it hit her. She'd watched a video of an alligator on social media one time. It made the same noise. Fresh waves of terror thundered throughout her insides, and she picked up her pace. Antonio had nothing on an alligator.

A third rumble made Sylvia hyperventilate as she continued down the path. Headlights flashed into her eyes, sending a pang through her insides.

As she hurried along the wooden pathway, her foot snagged on a piece of driftwood, sending her into a tumble. Her heart raced as she struggled to balance, but she fell sideways, hitting her temple against the handrail with a painful thud before crashing to the ground.

Louise held her hand over her chest. "Quick, get her up, son."

Manuel shined the flashlight over her body and let out a low growl. "I hope she's not dead. It'd be a shame to have made an enemy out of Antonio Morales for nothing."

He continued grumbling under his breath as he lifted Sylvia's limp body and carried her to the van.

# Chapter 23

The room spun around her like she was on the tilt-a-whirl, one of Sylvia's favorite rides at the county fair.

"Sweetheart?"

Sylvia licked her lips. "Mom?"

She heard someone sobbing. Was that Dad?

"You took a nasty fall, but the doctor says you'll be fine in no time."

Sylvia's eyes flew open. "Where are the boys?"

Mom blew her nose before answering. "They're with your Aunt Martha. We thought it was best for them to stay with her so they wouldn't hear anything about you on the news."

Some of the tension in Sylvia's shoulders faded. "Thank you."

"We love you so much." Dad said, kissing her hand. "Get some rest. Martha booked a flight to bring the boys home tomorrow afternoon."

Nodding her head slightly, her mind drifted away, and she couldn't fight the sleep that overtook her.

Early the following day, Cody Davenport from the CIA entered the hospital room.

He nodded at Dad before patting Mom's shoulder. Sylvia couldn't get over how much like Gareth he looked. Identical twins like her boys in almost every way.

"Did you know Lee Mason was alive before seeing him at the Morales compound?"

Sylvia shook her head, instantly regretting it. "No. I always believed he was, but I didn't know anything for sure."

He raised his eyebrow before firing off another question. "What made you believe he was alive?"

Sylvia rubbed her tender jaw from the fall. "The fact that his body was never found was my first clue."

Cody scribbled something in a notebook. "Did you know Antonio Morales on a personal level?"

"No. Of course not. Other than the few conversations we had during the trial."

More scribbling. "What about his daughter, Evangeline? Did you know her before the accident?"

She sighed and repositioned her leg under the cover. "No."

Cody fired off another question. "What about Kemena? Had you two ever met?"

"Absolutely not."

Despite her headache, Sylvia wanted to leave the hospital. "I'm sorry I haven't been of much help.

Antonio wanted me to replace his lost daughter. It was a strange coincidence."

Cody ran his hand through his black hair. "I appreciate you speaking with me. I may need to schedule a follow-up interview after you're home."

She took a sip of the sprite the nurse had brought her. "That's fine."

A little later, a knock sounded on the door. A woman poked her head inside the room. "Miss Sylvia?"

Sylvia raised up on her elbows. "Yes?"

"My name is Katherine Knight, and I'm a hospital counselor." Katherine's strawberry-blonde hair framed her kind green eyes. "I'd love to speak with you for a few minutes. Would that be okay?" Her warm demeanor put Sylvia at ease, making her an ideal grief counselor.

A faint smile appeared on Sylvia's lips as she nodded and said, "That will be fine."

After all that had happened, Sylvia may need a team of counselors.

# Chapter 24

Two weeks later, Sylvia found herself packing up her belongings while singing along to an upbeat tune. She needed to clear her head. The house she had shared with Lee would officially go on the market the next day. She and the boys would stay with her parents until they found a new place of their own.

She turned off the radio after the song finished. The local news and radio stations seemed unable to find anything newsworthy unless it involved Sylvia, Lee, or the Morales family.

Keatyn walked into Sylvia's bedroom. "You almost done?"

Sylvia flinched and grabbed her chest. "Oh goodness. You scared me."

"Sorry about that." Keatyn put her hands up. "I was letting you know I finished boxing the dishes up."

Sylvia put her hands on her hips and looked around the space. "I think we're almost done. Mom's coming tomorrow, and we can get the few things left."

"Okay, then, let's take a break." A mischievous grin skittered across Keatyn's face. "You hungry?"

A half smile appeared on Sylvia's face to hide the tightening in her chest. "I planned on eating supper with mom and dad. Wanna join us? Gareth and Lily are welcome to come."

"Thanks for the invite, but I better not tonight." Keatyn picked up her purse before meeting Sylvia's gaze. "You sure you don't want to grab something in town?"

"I'm positive," Sylvia said, tugging at a thread on her shirt. "Thank you for helping me, Keatyn."

Keatyn's eyes softened. "Anytime. Anything you need, call me. If you need me to, I can come back over tomorrow."

Sylvia's gaze bounced back and forth between Keatyn and the thread on her shirt. "Keatyn?"

"Yeah?" Keatyn answered as she set her purse back on the floor.

"Will you say an extra prayer for me?" Sylvia's words sounded like a fragile granny to her own ears. She cleared her throat, determined to be stronger.

"Of course." Keatyn's voice cracked as she continued.

Sylvia gazed out the window. "Let everyone at church know I appreciate their prayers. I have a card I plan to send. Instead, will you take it Sunday?"

"Yes." Keatyn stepped into Sylvia's line of sight. "When do you think you'll be back in service?"

"I'm not ready." Sylvia swallowed and glanced at the carpet. "I'll let you know."

Keatyn took Sylvia's hands in hers. "The longer you stay out, the harder it'll be to come back. I'm concerned for you because I love you."

"I know it, and I appreciate your concern. And I love you, too." Sylvia pushed on her churning stomach.

"We're all concerned." Keatyn let go of Sylvia's hands and dropped into a fold-up lawn chair. "People ask me constantly about you. You're very much loved by everyone."

Sylvia swallowed down the lump forming in her throat. "I know. They're good people. And can I get you to do one more thing for me?"

Keatyn hooked an arm over her raised knee. "You know it."

"Will you tell Alvin I'm sorry I haven't answered his calls?" Acid burned the back of her throat. "I need some time."

Keatyn slapped at a fly buzzing around her head before getting up and swatting it out the door. "Alvin understands. He's sorry he hasn't been able to see you or help you in any way."

"I appreciate him but need some time." Flaring her nostrils, Sylvia pressed between her brows. "I think those words are the only ones I ever say to him."

Lowering herself back into the chair, Keatyn nodded her agreement. "He's a good man and willing to give you time. Don't you realize after he's waited so long for you to deal with Lee's death? He's worried about you."

"I was going to file for a divorce but can't since Lee is legally dead." She dropped her eyes to the floor. "There's a lot of paperwork and hoops I'll be jumping through."

Keatyn's eyes bugged out. "I can imagine. I hate you have to go through this."

A long sigh escaped Sylvia. "I do, too. I've taken a leave of absence from work for a few weeks. To put Lee to rest. For good."

Keatyn's understanding tone washed over Sylvia. "That makes sense. You need time to heal. You've been through more than anyone should ever have to."

Sylvia massaged her temples. "I sometimes feel like I have more than I can handle."

Keatyn patted the seat beside her. "Sit by me for a minute. I want to tell you something I've figured out."

Syliva lowered herself into the fold-up chair next to Keatyn. "What's that?"

Keatyn pulled her phone out. "I met a lady on a plane last year who told me God said we would never have more than we can handle. At the time, I didn't know what to say to that statement."

Sylvia stared hard at Keatyn. "Well, do you think God does allow us to have more than we can handle?"

"I've studied because I needed to know for myself. I've concluded sometimes we absolutely do have more than we can handle. But do you know what else we have?"

Sylvia bit her bottom lip. "We have God. Right?"

Keatyn nodded. "That's right. We have a Heavenly Father Who makes ways for us to deal with those things that are too hard for us to handle on our own."

"That sounds right."

Keatyn scrolled through her online Bible app. "A couple of verses that stand out to me are in Proverbs chapter three. Verses five and six say, Trust in the Lord with all your heart, And lean not on your own understanding; In all your ways acknowledge Him, And He shall direct your paths."

"I see where we must trust God even when we fear things will turn out worse than we can imagine. Without God, I don't know how I'd get through all this." Sylvia looked out the window, her eyes landing on the boys' swing. "You know, I didn't know if I'd get past being whipped like an animal. But I try not to think about it."

Keatyn squeezed Sylvia's hand. "God also gives us people who love us, people we can lean upon for strength and love. People like Gareth and me. Our church family. But especially people like Alvin."

"I know, and I appreciate you all so much." Sylvia shifted in her seat, ready to change the subject. "I'd like to continue this study with you when I'm feeling more focused. Does that sound good?"

Keatyn's face lit up as she spoke. "You bet it does. I'm ready whenever you are."

"I'll let you know." Sylvia squeezed her eyes shut. "Hey, before you leave, will you let me get the stuff out of the garage?"

"Absolutely." Keatyn pushed herself out of the chair. "I'll help with whatever you need."

A car door slamming out front interrupted their conversation. Keatyn pulled back the curtain and sighed. "It's Cordelia."

Cordelia paused in the doorway. "I brought you two some brownies. The sun's setting, so I figured y'all would want a snack."

Sylvia lifted a brownie to her mouth and bit a chunk off. "This is what I needed, thank you."

Cordelia inclined her head toward the front door. "You're welcome! You have another visitor pulling up."

"Oh?" Sylvia washed the brownie down with a sip of iced tea. "Who?"

Keatyn snapped the blinds closed. "Just my lug of a brother."

# Chapter 25

A wave of panic seized Sylvia's chest when Alvin walked in wearing a pink Adidas t-shirt and black joggers. If she planned to stay away from him, she needed to take drastic action.

He flashed a smile—the kind that made Sylvia's stomach flutter and her anxiety heighten. "Can I talk to you outside for a minute, Sylvia?"

Pushing aside the fluttering in her stomach, Sylvia nodded. "I want to get home before dark."

Why had she said that?

Because her nerves bounced in her chest, and she had no idea what else to say.

Remain calm. Take deep breaths.

Alvin ran a hand through his hair, his gaze fixed on Sylvia as she nervously fiddled with her own hair, eyes dropping to the floor.

Despite her efforts to push him away, he remained a constant presence in her life.

Since Lee's death, he had followed her around like a puppy, waiting for her to notice him. Though she cared for him, she had fought those feelings.

Now, however, her life had taken a turn for the worse. She was no longer a grieving widow. At this point, she was a scorned woman, destined to be talked about forever.

And now that Lee had been found alive, their relationship would end. For good.

If only things were different.

"Okay. Let's sit in my truck. I left the air on." After settling in his truck, Alvin opened his mouth to speak, but Sylvia beat him to it.

"Alvin, I hope you'll accept my apology." She couldn't keep her traitorous cheeks from reddening.

Alvin switched the air down a notch and kept his eyes looking out the window. "You have nothing to apologize for."

"You and I both know better than that." She pressed her back against the door and met Alvin's gaze. "I've kept you dangling for a very long time, and I'm sorry. If I hadn't, you could've already been married, starting a life with a wife and maybe even a kid on the way."

Alvin's face pinched. "I have a life. And I won't let you harbor some false blame."

"But, I've led you on. I know I have." Sylvia sucked in a breath and held it.

Throwing out a dismissing wave of his hand, he balked. "I'm a big boy. I could've moved on at any given time. That's on me. Not you."

As Sylvia released her breath, her chest relaxed. "You know why I did it, don't you?"

He shrugged before cutting his eyes at her. His lips lifted into a grin. "My overall charming nature and extraordinarily handsome good looks?"

"Absolutely," Sylvia answered with a small laugh.

For two heartbeats, she thought about how life with him and the boys would be, but she pushed those thoughts aside.

They only hurt her.

Maybe Keatyn was right, and she was a glutton for punishment.

Turning in his seat, Alvin bit his lip. "But seriously, I want you to know I'll support your marriage to Lee and do whatever you need to help bring him to the gospel." He took a breath and fixed his gaze on her face. "When will he be home?"

All humor gone, Sylvia's mouth twisted into a frown. "I don't guess Keatyn filled you in?"

His lips drew down into a frown. "After I heard Lee was found alive, all Keatyn said was it's not her story to tell."

"Only a few people know what really happened." Sylvia pushed on her chest with her fist. "Lee –"

Sitting straight up, Alvin put his hand out. "Hey, hey, you don't have to tell me anything until you're ready."

She closed her eyes briefly before meeting Alvin's concerned gaze. "Lee faked his own death so he could be with another woman. Oh, and not just any woman. A vicious mob boss meaner than her crime lord father."

Darkness passed Alvin's features. "I'm so sorry."

She tapped her foot so hard her knee bounced. "So, Lee and I will divorce as soon as possible. I don't know how that works since he's already remarried. But you better believe I'll be figuring it out."

Alvin took a big gulp of his drink. "I don't know what to say. Other than Lee Mason is a fool."

"Maybe it was my fault." She shrugged. "Either way, I won't be dating anyone as a divorcee. Ever again."

Alvin snapped his gaze away. "What Lee did wasn't your fault. Anyone that knew you could tell you were a good wife."

Her face hardened. "I can't take that chance. I won't take that chance. I'm bad news, Alvin. It'll be in your best interest to move on and leave me alone."

How could she ever make Alvin happy if she wasn't even woman enough to keep her husband?

Maybe Lee realized how much of a failure she was once he met Kemena.

Would Alvin end up feeling the same way?

Alvin attempted to argue. "Hold on a minute. You're getting divorced because Lee committed adultery. How is that your fault?"

With one last look at Alvin's face, Sylvia opened the door and stepped out. She paused and leaned around the door. "I won't be dating you or anyone else. Please respect my wishes."

As soon as Alvin backed out, a masked figure emerged from the shadows and circled around the house, his sights set on Sylvia.

# Chapter 26

A faint scream echoed nearby. Alvin pressed the brakes and scanned the area. His heart raced when he checked the rearview mirror.

A masked man had Sylvia pinned to the ground. Alvin's instincts kicked into high gear like he was overseas in enemy territory. Slamming the gear into park, he sprinted towards Sylvia with his handgun drawn.

He slowed down to see if he could take a shot, but the attacker had Sylvia on the ground, leaving Alvin no room for a clear shot.

Alvin glimpsed Cordelia and Keatyn running out the front door. Cordelia had her phone up to her ear, and Keatyn pulled a gun from her purse. That's all he needed. Keatyn accidentally shooting Sylvia.

Alvin dove on top of the man, dragging him off Sylvia. Alvin's eyes darted to where she lay, still and quiet. Blood rushed through his chest, settling in the pit of his stomach. He let out a roar and slammed his fist into the side of the man's head.

Sirens sounded in the distance. Alvin leveled his gun at the man, ready to shoot. In the blink of an eye, the man knocked the gun out of Alvin's hand, and it flew into a bush.

The man then took his feet and kicked Alvin in the chest. Alvin crashed against Keatyn's Infiniti, hitting her side mirror. A sharp pinch exploded from his eye socket. He wiped the blood drizzling into his eye with his shirt. The attacker wasted no time trying to get the upper hand. He grabbed Alvin by the throat.

Stars clouded Alvin's vision. He reached for the switchblade knife he kept in his pocket, clicked the button, and the blade shot open. The attacker's grip increased in intensity as Alvin plunged the knife into the man's side. The man grabbed his side and met Alvin's gaze.

A woman with long dark hair slowly approached Sylvia. Alvin's body tensed when the woman put a gun to Sylvia's head.

She leveled dark eyes on Alvin. "Let my husband go, or I'll shoot."

The man tensed and jerked away from Alvin, holding his side where Alvin had stabbed him. "Kemena. I said we would not be killing the mother of my children."

The breath almost strangled in Alvin's throat. So, this was Lee? How did he not recognize the man he played football with as a kid? Had he truly changed that much after his so-called death?

The sirens grew louder. Lee hobbled over to Kemena and grabbed her arm. He relieved her of the gun and pointed it at Alvin. He kept the gun aimed at Alvin's head until they disappeared behind the house.

Cordelia and Keatyn rushed to Sylvia's side as an ambulance, and two police cars slid into the driveway.

A few minutes later, Alvin climbed into the ambulance. "Hey. You doing all right?"

Sylvia's brown eyes shimmered with tears. "I don't know how I'm doing. My husband tried to... what? Kidnap me? Kill me?"

Alvin's lips turned downward. "I don't think he was trying to kill you. I believe he and that woman wanted to kidnap you for leverage?"

Sylvia closed her eyes and rubbed her neck. "Leverage for what?"

He shrugged. "That's a good question. Only time will tell."

She shifted in her seat before taking a deep breath. "Thank you for saving me. Are you hurt?"

His breath quickened, and he had to swallow his heart to keep it from bursting. No call to think she meant anything more than a simple thank you. "No, I'm not hurt too badly. I'll be fine. I'd do anything for you, Sylvia. Face any hurt. Don't you realize that by now?"

"I appreciate that. But nothing's changed." She dropped her eyes to her hands before looking at

Alvin dead in the face. "If anything, I'm more determined to stay away from you than ever."

Alvin's jaw clenched, and he fought the urge to scream. "That's ridiculous."

"Can't you see? My life is too complicated, and I'm starting to think it's all my fault." Tears welled up in her eyes as she covered her mouth with her hand.

He reached his hand out and wiped her tears. "Please stop blaming yourself. Let me help you through this."

She shook her head, bolted out of her seat, and through the back of the ambulance. Never once looking back.

# Chapter 27

No matter what she tried to think about, Sylvia couldn't get her mind off Lee trying to kidnap her. What had happened to the man she'd married? After the failed attempt, he and Kemena disappeared.

The doorbell ringing interrupted her thoughts. Mom dashed out of the kitchen and opened the door.

A look of surprise flashed across Mom's face as she stepped aside to let the three elders from the church in. "Well, hello, gentlemen. This is a nice surprise."

Rodney Willis first shook her hand, followed by Randall Patterson, then Daniel Bradford. The three men couldn't be more different.

Rodney was in his late fifties with a head full of red hair. Randall had to be pushing seventy, had a round belly, and kept his head shaved bald. Daniel was in his sixties, was skinny as a green bean, and had dark skin and curly white hair. But they all displayed the love of God.

Dad had told Sylvia how impressed Mom was with the way the elders treated others while Sylvia was missing.

The elders not only helped with food and the search but also took the time to pray with Edgar and her.

Good afternoon, Mrs. Jane. We wanted to stop by and say hello and check on your family." Daniel said.

"We're doing so much better now that Sylvia is home." She pointed at the living area. "Please, make yourselves comfortable. Would you like something to drink?"

They each claimed a seat but declined a drink.

Daniel glanced at Sylvia. "And how are you? We've missed seeing you and the boys."

"I'm on my way to recovery." She swiveled around and waved at Rhyland and Oakland, playing in the pool with her dad. "I asked Keatyn to tell everyone how much I appreciate the prayers and all that was done for my family while I was away."

"She told us, and we read the card you sent. But that's not the same as seeing you in person," Rodney added.

Sylvia's eyes darted around the room. "I know."

Randall shifted in his seat. "Can we do anything for you, Sylvia? Or for you, Mrs. Jane?"

"Not that we can think of," Mom replied.

Rodney crossed his legs. "Tanya and I enjoyed getting to know you and your good husband. We wish it had been under better circumstances."

Mom beamed, "Yes. We did as well."

Daniel nodded. "My wife said the same thing. We should all get together soon. Or better yet, y'all could come to visit us at church Sunday and eat lunch with us afterward."

"I'll have to ask Ed."

Randall stood up. "Why don't we go ask him ourselves? Would that be all right with you?"

A wave of relief crossed Mom's face. She must be confident Dad would tell them no. "That's fine with me."

Rodney stayed inside while Randall and Daniel made their way to the pool. They talked for a few minutes until everyone came inside.

Randall's grin couldn't have gotten any wider as he met Mom's gaze. "Ed's agreed to come to service Sunday. We can't wait to see you all there."

Mom kept a smile plastered on her face as they said goodbye to their visitors. As soon as the door closed behind them, she turned to Dad. "What are you thinking?"

Dad's unblinking gaze met Mom's surprised one. "I was thinking these are good people, and I want to get to know them better."

"Well, I'm not going with you."

"Yes, you are. I told them we'd both be there." He pecked her on the lips, "and we will."

# Chapter 28

Three weeks. Sylvia had missed three weeks of sermons. Three weeks of Bible study. Of singing. Of fellowship.

So why was it so hard to get out of the vehicle?

Mom would only agree to come for the sermon, so they missed the morning Bible study. That meant she had less time to be nervous. Less time to see Alvin.

Even the turmoil flowing through Sylvia couldn't stop her heart from singing as her parents entered the church building. Despite her joy at seeing her parents in service, Sylvia's insides rolled like the washing machine on a heavy-duty cycle.

Facing Alvin wouldn't be an easy task.

Turning to speak to Lunell Bradford, she lost sight of her parents for a second. Her heart almost stopped dead in her chest when she laid eyes on them. The reason for her nervousness just so happened to be standing with her parents and the boys. Alvin. She took a deep breath and headed in their direction.

Alvin stepped to the front pew and took a seat before Sylvia reached them. She wasn't sure if she was happy, sad, or mad. But what should you expect when you tell someone to leave you alone? Flowers and candy?

When it was time for the sermon, Sylvia's eyes almost popped out of their sockets when Alvin went to the pulpit instead of Gareth.

Keatyn turned slightly in her seat and smiled at Sylvia. She smiled back before putting her complete focus on Alvin.

Alvin laid some papers down on the podium and opened up his Bible. "I want to thank the elders for allowing me to preach this morning." He met Gareth's eyes and smiled. "And Gareth for willingly stepping aside so I can. Now, I also may need to apologize to the rest of y'all. This is my first time preaching, so y'all are my guinea pigs."

Laughter sounded from some of the church members. "When I started thinking about preaching, I asked myself some questions. The first one I asked was, have I counted the cost of discipleship? Because, if not, I need to study what I must do as a member before I could ever consider delivering a sermon."

He flipped the pages in his Bible. "Turn with me to Matthew 6:33. Let's read it together."

*"But seek first the kingdom of God and His righteous-ness, and all these things shall be added to you."*

"This is a command we all must follow. Whether we are teachers, preachers, members, elders, or deacons does not matter. The list could go on and on. The command is given to every one of us."

"Seeking first the kingdom of God and His right-eousness means God must come before all else. He must be the priority in all of life's choices. Everything else must revolve around our Father, and nothing, and I mean absolutely nothing else, can be allowed to interfere with my seeking Him and His righteous-ness."

"God will not force us to be his disciple. He has given us free will. Read Matthew 16:24-27 with me."

*"Then Jesus said to His disciples, "If anyone desires to come after Me, let him deny himself, and take up his cross, and follow Me. For whoever desires to save his life will lose it, but whoever loses his life for My sake will find it. For what profit is it to a man if he gains the whole world, and loses his own soul? Or what will a man give in exchange for his soul? For the Son of Man will come in the glory of His Father with His angels, and then He will reward each according to his works."*

"If anyone wants to follow me, this indicates a de-cision must be made. Are you making that decision moment by moment, hour by hour, day by day?"

Alvin scanned the pews, allowing his eyes to rest on each section for a second. "Many claim they want to live for God, but when faced with the demands on their time, talents, and finances, they change their minds. Like the rich young ruler in Matthew 19:22, they often walk away sorrowfully, unwilling to give God what is rightfully His."

After meeting Alvin's eyes, Sylvia struggled to hear anything but her own heartbeat.

Alvin's voice intensified as he concluded the sermon. "To follow me means to walk, talk, live, serve, and love as He did. Carrying our cross daily is about love and devotion. Do you have what it takes to be a disciple of Christ? If not, what will you do about it?"

As soon as the last song ended, Sylvia rushed out the front door.

# Chapter 29

Later that day, Sylvia pulled into a guest parking space at the church on Breakwater Avenue and killed the engine. It would be best for her and the boys to attend evening service elsewhere. Anywhere that Alvin wasn't.

"Awe, mom. Why are we going here?" Rhyland glanced out the window and huffed.

"I want to go to our church. I like it there." Oakland made sure Sylvia had his two cents as well.

Sylvia fixed her face to the most upbeat she could muster. "It doesn't hurt to try new things and visit new places, right? It'll be fun."

Both Rhyland and Oakland crossed their arms and gave Sylvia the stink eye.

She pooched her bottom lip out. "Come on, work with me. Pretty please."

"Okay." Oakland gave in first. "I guess."

Rhyland glared at Oakland. "Traitor." He cut his eyes at Sylvia. "I want to go see Mr. Alvin and Lily."

Sylvia's tone turned firm. "Well, we're going here this evening, and that's that. Now apologize to your brother for calling him a name and get out of the car."

"Yes, ma'am." His head dropped. "I'm sorry, Oakland."

The twins' birthday was in a few months, and Sylvia sometimes wondered if they would be six or twenty-six. Some days, they acted like kids, and on others, they spoke like grown-ups.

Two older gentlemen opened the double doors when they stepped on the sidewalk. One was tall and skinny with gray hair and pale skin; the other was of medium height and complexion with gray hair and wire-rimmed glasses.

The taller one spoke up first. "Welcome to Breakwater! I'm Kenneth Howell, and this here is my partner in crime, Hillard Harrison."

Sylvia smiled and introduced herself and the boys. Upon entering the foyer, they were greeted by several different people.

The congregation may have been smaller, but the people were friendly—all except one older woman in a wheelchair. Sylvia smiled and waved at her, but the woman just stared at Sylvia. Walking past the rude woman, Sylvia claimed an empty pew.

After the closing prayer, Sylvia stood up to leave when someone touched her arm. She turned and greeted a woman close to her age. "Hello."

The woman stuck her hand out. "Hi, I'm Brinley Miller."

Sylvia shook her hand. Brinley? Hopefully, not the one that went on a date with Alvin. "Nice to meet you, Brinley."

Hillard Harrison wheeled the rude woman up. "Miss Sylvia, this is my wife, Susan." He leaned close to Susan's ear. "Honey, we have some visitors. Sylvia and her twin boys Rhyland and Oakland."

The corners of Susan's mouth lifted, and she held her hand out. "Hello, there. We're so happy you came our way."

Sylvia took her hand. "We're happy to be here. It's nice meeting you."

Susan squeezed her hand. "Please come back and see us. We love visitors."

"We'll sure try, Mrs. Susan." Sylvia's lips rose, but her insides trembled with shame. Shame that she judged Susan as rude before even giving her a chance. Susan was blind, not hateful.

"Can I speak to you outside?" Brinley broke Sylvia's concentration on what she'd done.

Sylvia cocked her head. "Sure. What's going on?"

They stepped through the double doors and over to Sylvia's SUV. Brinley eyeballed Sylvia. "I recognized you as the woman who –"

Sylvia cleared her throat and shook her head. The boys had no idea what had happened to Sylvia, and she planned to keep it that way.

Oakland interrupted. "Mom, I need to use the bathroom."

"The bathroom is inside the front door to the left," Brinley said.

Sylvia leaned on the side of her SUV. "Okay, Rhyland, you go with him."

Brinley waited until the boys were out of earshot. "I realized that you know Alvin Griffin when I saw you. Am I correct in that assumption?"

Sylvia bristled. "Why do you ask?"

"I ask because he and I went on a couple of dates, but he never could focus on getting to know me." Brinley narrowed her eyes. "Turns out he's in love with someone else."

Pressing her lips tight, Sylvia's chin tilted to the left. "What does that have to do with me?"

"I think you already know." Brinley massaged her temples. "Look, you probably think this is none of my business, but Alvin and I have become friends. And I don't like to see my friends hurt."

Sylvia opened her mouth, but Brinley held up her hand. "That man loves you with all his heart. I'm sorry if I seem rude or out of line. But I wanted you to know he's hurting because of your situation."

Sylvia understood why Brinley felt the need to say those things. But understanding didn't make them any easier to hear.

The boys came running up, laughing at something they did in the bathroom.

Sylvia opened the back door and pointed for the boys to hop in. "I appreciate you letting me know, but you don't know the whole situation. Have a good night, Brinley."

Brinley's lips formed a thin line. "You too, Sylvia. Don't wait until it's too late."

Back in the car, those six words swam around in Sylvia's mind.

*Don't wait until it's too late.*

# Chapter 30

The stars shined bright in the purple and navy sky over Pensacola Beach, casting a soft glow on the three men. Alvin shifted his weight to his left leg as he waited for Cody Davenport to speak.

"Thanks for meeting me." Cody ran his hand over his newly shaved head.

"No problem." Gareth Davenport glanced at Alvin. "We figured something was up, or you wouldn't have asked to meet us here."

Cody sighed. "Earlier today, Lee and Kemena Mason were found in a hotel in the US Virgin Islands."

"So, you have them in custody?" Alvin asked.

"They don't, or we wouldn't be here," Gareth replied.

"They weren't going down without a fight. Lee Mason fired on the group attempting to take them into custody. It didn't end well."

Cody paused and stared at the stars. After a few seconds, he continued. "After a standoff and shootout, Lee's body was recovered in the hotel room. We also lost a team member, and another is in critical condition."

Gareth leaned in. "I'm so sorry. Was Kemena in the hotel?"

Cody pressed his lips tightly. "Once again, she eluded capture."

Gareth's eyebrows raised. "Was she there to begin with?"

A couple walked by with intertwined hands, gasping and giggling at the sky. Cody waited until they were out of earshot before answering. "She's on camera there."  He lowered his voice to a whisper. "Gareth, I think we have a mole in the department."

"You've told me that before." Gareth matched Cody's tone. "Do you have any hard proof?"

Cody's eyes narrowed to slits. "I think it goes way up the ladder. Higher than we know. But you need to stay away from this one. I shouldn't have opened my mouth."

Gareth waved his hand. "It's fine. I'll pray for your team member and for the situation."

"I appreciate it." Cody popped a piece of mint gum into his mouth before continuing. "The main reason I asked to meet is to ask you and Alvin to be the ones to break the news to Lee's wife. After all she's been through, I'd hate for her to get a phone call from a stranger."

Alvin shook his head. "Thank you."

Cody gave a brief nod before he started to walk away. Gareth laid his hand on Cody's arm. "I'd like to see you in service, you know."

"I know. I'm working on it, brother." He replied.

Sylvia stepped onto the front porch and stared at the dark sky. Gareth and Keatyn pulled into the drive.

After inviting them in and settling on the back porch, Sylvia smiled nervously at Keatyn. "I have a bad feeling about this meeting. So go ahead and lay whatever it is on me."

Keatyn grimaced and cast a glance at Gareth, who took the lead. "Sylvia, we got some news about Lee tonight."

Scooting closer to Sylvia, Keatyn spoke softly. "Everyone involved thought we should be the ones to come by."

"Lee's dead, isn't he?" Sylvia croaked out.

"We're so sorry, but yes." Keatyn pulled Sylvia close.

Gareth patted Sylvia's hand. "Would you like me to bring your parents out?

Sylvia watched the mesmerizing pink lights in the pool, nodding slowly.

After spending nearly three hours with her family, Gareth and Keatyn left at midnight.

Sylvia and her parents sat in the living room, grieving the loss of Sylvia's husband once again, but this time it was for real.

*Chapter 31*

A soft breeze carried a child's laughter as Sylvia sipped her coffee beside the pool. She had her parents' place to herself for a few hours while they took the boys to a birthday party. They'd offered to take the boys to give Sylvia time alone to process what had happened.

Time that was much needed. A sob started in her gut, building up to a wail escaping her chest.

How could Lee do this to her?

To their boys?

How?

He'd always sworn Sylvia was his life after everything he'd gone through as a kid.

Lee had been born to a single woman who spent more time trying to find the next great man than she did with her son. He lived with friends and on the street after his mom died at the young age of forty.

A police officer took him under his wing, and that's how he got started in law enforcement. He and Sylvia met in her second year of college and married shortly after.

It had been a happy time for Sylvia. She thought it had been for Lee as well. She thought they were in love. That their marriage would last forever. The birth of the twin boys completed their family. Life had been good.

Then Lee had supposedly died before the boys were even four years old. That was the hardest thing Sylvia had ever faced. Losing her first love nearly broke her. A sharp pain shot through her heart, and she doubled over.

Without her parents, Sylvia would have found things much harder. They helped by picking up the boys so she could work and avoid daycare. Their support had been invaluable.

She had Lee buried him in the plot she'd purchased the first time he "died." They'd have a memorial to honor his life a little later.

What would she do now? Allowing Lee's deceit to destroy her wasn't an option. She needed to lean on God more now than ever.

Maybe it was time for her to get away from Pensacola for a while. She took a sip of her black coffee and sat the mug on the table.

Mom came up behind Sylvia and rubbed her shoulders. "Honey, you should go visit with your cousins and Aunt Martha at Tybee. Dad and I'll go with you."

"You know what, mom? That's the best thing you've said all week." Sylvia picked up her phone and typed up a message to Keatyn.

Two hours later, with flights booked for the following morning, they zipped around the house, preparing for their trip.

Excitement buzzed through Sylvia for the first time since she had discovered Lee's death.

She prayed the feeling would last.

# Chapter 32

The first Sunday morning in Tybee was a day Sylvia had looked forward to. Meeting new people always brightened her spirits, and she hoped today would be no different.

She finished applying her makeup after breakfast and called for the boys to brush their teeth.

As she left her bedroom, Mom stepped into her line of sight. Sylvia tilted her head. "Where are you going?"

She pulled a loose curl behind her ear. "Are you not going to church this morning?"

"Of course I am," Sylvia replied. "Wait. Are you going with me?"

Dad chuckled. "We all are baby girl."

"The entire family?" Sylvia clasped her hands together. "Are you serious?"

"Close your mouth, dear. Unless you want Oakland to put a bug in it." Martha grimaced.

"Mama speaks from experience," Lisa said in between giggles. Martha raised her eyebrow at Lisa, and it made the laughs worse. She did attempt to cover her full, red lips with her hand to calm herself down, to no avail.

Lisa inherited her daddy's long legs and hair, whereas her mama was short in stature. Her skin sparkled so white Martha had asked if they'd switched her daughter with another baby in the hospital. Turns out she'd inherited her daddy's skin tone.

"Sis tells the truth. I saw it with my own eyes. I thought mama was gonna die." Lisa's brother, Theo, added.

Oakland raised off the sofa and looked at Martha with a straight face. "I'm telling y'all it was Rhyland."

There wasn't a person in the house able to contain their laughter.

A few hours later, after church, they sat around two tables pushed together at Salty's Shrimp House with the preacher and his family.

Lisa was sweet on the preacher's son, Beau, and had been attending church with him the past few months.

"I enjoyed your sermon, Arlie." Mom said before taking a bite of buttered bread.

"Yes, I'd never considered the Fruit of the Spirit as being singular or looked at it that way until today," Martha added.

"There's power in the gospel," Arlie replied.

Their server brought their plates out, and the conversation moved on to what made Arlie pursue preaching before they started telling funny stories.

Theo had the group in tears over the bug situation. He'd told the story twice already.

Arlie's eyes crinkled around the corners. "It's been a blessing getting to know your family."

"We feel the same way," Dad replied. "To tell the truth, Jane and I haven't attended service in over twenty years until recently." His eyes settled on Sylvia.

Warmth entered Sylvia's heart, and a thought struck. Her parents had never taken her to church. Mom had always refused to even discuss attending.

Until now.

Until after she was kidnapped.

Could this be the reason she'd been looking for?

Had it been right there in front of her this entire time?

Everything that happened to her wasn't for nothing.

Her parents had been to church with her twice in the past few weeks.

She left the restaurant with a few new friends and a whole new outlook.

# Chapter 33

Although Alvin hadn't seen Sylvia in weeks, he couldn't shake her from his heart. He longed to hold her, comfort her, and offer her strength.

But her consistent refusal to see how much he cared had become increasingly difficult to handle. Could he break through the wall she had built between them? Should he even continue to try?

He pedaled the bicycle with all his strength, the muscles in his legs straining as he raced against the morning breeze.

The sun began to rise over Pensacola Beach, its light casting a warm glow across the sky. Captivated by the stunning vista, he pulled over, unable to resist the allure of the breathtaking scene before him.

He unstrapped his water bottle, taking a refreshing swig as he breathed in the salty air.

The resounding words of the hymn "How Great Thou Art" filled Alvin's thoughts as the sunrise unfolded before him. The sky transformed into a breathtaking canvas, where brilliant hues of orange, pink, and gold intertwined, creating a mesmerizing display.

Each moment brought a new depth to the colors as they swirled and blended seamlessly, painting a picture that never failed to leave Alvin in awe.

The sheer beauty of the dawn's light captured his heart, and he found himself lost in its artistry, grateful for the daily reminder of nature's splendor.

The Lord had been so merciful and generous to create such beauty for man to have access to. He bowed his head and gave thanks.

He thought back to his last tour of duty with the Navy and very different view.

Their truck had been forced off the road, and they went tumbling down a mountainside. This fall could have killed them all, but their team was protected.

The worst injury happened to his friend, Greg Watson, who lost an arm. Alvin broke his leg in three places, but they both survived.

He'd been so thankful to be allowed to come home, even with a limp.

His longing to marry Sylvia and raise the boys had gotten him through many desperate times while overseas.

After his leg injury, he decided to leave military life behind. Alvin found it challenging to be content in whatever state, like the apostle Paul.

He wanted a wife, someone to share life with. Maybe he had been forcing the issue instead of relying on God.

As a small cloud skidded across the sky, Alvin blew out a breath. Wow.

Maybe God had a different timeline than Alvin. It was time for Alvin to wait on God to send him a mate in His time. Not Alvin's.

His phone buzzing interrupted his line of thought. It was a message from Brinley.

> *Hey!*

> *Hey, Brinley. Kinda early – you ok?*

> *Yes! I've been on a run. But I wanted to tell you Darren asked me out. Are you okay with that?*

> *Absolutely! He and I spoke about it, and I wish you the best*

> *That means so much!*

> *Have a good day, Brin.*

> *You too. Hey. One more thing…don't give up on Sylvia. I know she loves you.*

Alvin had to read the last message several times.

*How in the world would you know that?*

*Women's intuition. Trust me, and don't lose hope.*

Shaking off the conversation, he stepped into the warm water, the gentle waves lapping around his legs.

With a deep breath, he dove beneath the surface, surrendering to the refreshing embrace of the ocean.

After thirty minutes of gliding through the water, he retrieved his bicycle, ready for the scenic ride back to his cottage.

Early the next morning, Gareth and Alvin drove to the docks for a day of deep-sea fishing. They'd planned a fish fry at Gareth's and had invited several friends over that evening.

Alvin looked forward to it. He wished Sylvia-

He stopped the thought as soon as it entered his mind.  He had to stop wishing for things and start spending more time praying for God's will to be done. Then have faith that it'll work out for the best.

As soon as he boarded the boat, the pungent aroma of bleach mixed with fish hit Alvin. He shook the captain's hand. "Did your cleaning service double up on the Clorox this time, Cap?"

"Cleaning service? This ain't the Ritz, young'un." Captain Dougal McGuire waved around the boat with a beefy arm.

Dougal had come to the United States from Scotland when he was fourteen to live with his aunt after his parents died. His formerly red hair had hints of gray, but his beard and mustache were as red as when he was a youngster. He and Dad met in school, and they'd been good friends ever since.

Dougal chuckled then his eyes landed on Gareth. "How's that gorgeous wife of yours?"

"Keatyn's doing great." Gareth shook Dougal's hand. "She's working hard to open a restaurant on a boat someday."

"Wonderful news." Dougal rubbed his protruding belly. "Keep me posted, and I'll be her first customer."

Gareth pulled the shirt he had on top of his t-shirt off. "We sure will."

Even though it took two hours to get far enough out for deep sea fishing Alvin's spirits were high with the thought of the day ahead.

He and Gareth invited all the customers to church, and a couple said they'd be there Sunday. A few avoided them, but it didn't hurt their feelings.

Alvin reeled in two Mahi Mahi, and Gareth caught three Whitefish despite the sharks following the boat.

"What time is it?" Someone asked from behind Alvin.

Alvin took his phone out and let them know it was almost noon. Before he could put it back into his pocket, it slipped out of his hand.

He leaned over the rail to grab his phone, but it was out of reach. Placing his hand on his forehead, he half groaned, half sighed as his phone plunged into the dark water.

He stared after it for a minute before shrugging. "Well, at least the sharks have something to call home with."

# Chapter 34

D ue to the perfect weather, the flight landed in Pensacola exactly on schedule. Sylvia
hummed a tune as she fished for her keys in her
pocket.

After spending a few weeks in Tybee, she had
finally decided it was time to be open and honest
with Alvin about her feelings.

But what if he was no longer interested?

He could be footloose and fancy-free with another woman on his arm.

That thought caused a fleeting scowl.

She stopped herself.

Think positive thoughts. Holding her breath, she
dialed Alvin's cell phone number. The scowl reap-
peared when it went straight to voicemail.

Time to go see Keatyn. She'd know what to do.

And it didn't hurt that Alvin lives on the same
street as Keatyn.

With a plan in place, Sylvia pulled out of the airport and headed to Pensacola Beach.

She cringed when she recalled her last conversation with Alvin, where she had asked him to leave her alone. She never imagined she would actually become a widow—this time for real.

It was a bit surreal how drastically her life had changed.

Not that she was happy Lee had been killed. On the contrary, her heart was saddened.

He'd been her husband. He was the father of her boys, and they'd been happy. Or so she had thought. She hated he'd died in such a terrible way. But everything that happened to Lee was because of the decisions he made.

Even though she was sad, she couldn't dwell on the past. And that's what Lee was. The past. Praying for God's guidance and for His will to be done, she decided to think about something else.

As Sylvia arrived at Keatyn's place, she noticed cars parked all around the two-story teal and white beach house.

She followed the sound of laughter coming from the backyard and took the path leading to the beach area.

She made it to the edge of the sand when a woman's loud voice rang out. "I'm so glad Brinley found such a good man."

Cordelia spoke next. "Me too, Diane. They hit it off rather quickly, didn't they?"

"Yes, they did. She always looked for a military man, so someone from the Navy is such a perfect fit."

Sylvia's bones turned to ice as she unintentionally eavesdropped, but she couldn't pull herself away from the conversation.

"So, is he marriage material?" Cordelia asked.

"Oh, I have no doubt. That man's smitten already." The other woman replied.

A tightening sensation hit Sylvia's chest as she glanced at the beach. From where she stood, it looked like Gareth and Keatyn sat around a fire with Kyle and Rebecca.

Her line of sight moved to people playing volley-ball, and she froze.

Her arms fell limply to her sides, and her body deflated.

Alvin and Brinley were clearly having a great time together. And why shouldn't they be? Sylvia had made it clear there was no chance for them to be together before she left for Tybee.

Turning on her heel, she walked to her car and drove away. Her vision blurred, and for the first time since escaping Antonio Morales, she screamed in agony.

It was dark by the time Sylvia reached her parents' house. Dreading the prospect of spending the night alone, she gazed at the stars through the sunroof, contemplating her next move.

Just then, her sixth-grade teacher, Mrs. Barriga, pulled into the driveway next door and waved at

Sylvia. She grabbed a bag from the back seat of her Ford Taurus and placed it on the hood before walking over.

"What are you doing, dear?" Mrs. Barriga craned her neck to look into the back of the SUV. "Where's everybody else?

Placing both hands on the steering wheel, Sylvia sighed. "Oh, trying to decide if I want to go inside or not. I'm the only one who came home from Georgia today."

"Hmmm." Mrs. Barriga stuck the tip of her tongue on the side of her thin lips. "I have a box of brownie mix in that bag over there. Why don't you spend the night at the house with me?"

Sylvia grinned and put her hand on the door handle. "I haven't stayed at your house since I was ten or eleven."

Mrs. Barriga headed toward her car. "Come on inside."

"Yes, ma'am." Sylvia replied as she got out of the car, hoping to drown her sorrows in chocolate.

# Chapter 35

The next morning, Sylvia nearly drove past Fort Hill on her way to attend the service at Breakwater. But she decided it would be better to confront Alvin sooner rather than later since she couldn't avoid him forever, especially with his sister being her best friend.

Rebecca opened the door for Sylvia, hugged her, and handed her a bulletin. "I thought you were in Georgia," she said.

Sylvia shook her head. "I decided to come on home early."

Keatyn marched up to Sylvia and linked their arms together. "Why didn't you tell me you were home? When did you get back?"

"And where are those precious boys?" Tanya Willis added as she walked into the building.

"Well, I came home yesterday. I planned on sur-prising everyone." Sylvia looked at Tanya. "The boys stayed in Georgia with my parents."

"I wish I'd known." Keatyn looked at Sylvia side-ways. "We had a party at the house last night. You could've come."

Before Sylvia could answer, Keatyn's daughter, Lily, tripped and hit her head on the corner of a hallway table. Keatyn rushed over and picked Lily up, followed by Rebecca, who was an RN.

They disappeared into Gareth's office, and Sylvia continued into the auditorium.

It didn't take two seconds for the moment she'd been dreading to happen.

Alvin stood in the aisle, chatting with his dad and stepmother, Myles and Cordelia Griffin.

Sylvia's stomach dropped when he met her gaze. The teal of his shirt accentuated the sparkle in his eyes, causing her heart to beat harder, if that were possible.

Cordelia waved her over. Sylvia groaned.

This couldn't get any more awkward.

"Sylvia." Cordelia wrapped her arms around Sylvia and screamed in her ear. Cordelia had a bad habit of leaving her hearing aids at home. "It's so good to see you."

"Hello. It's good to see you all, as well." Sylvia replied as she returned Cordelia's hug.

Chuckling, Myles put his hand up like he was shar-ing a big secret. "Del left her hearing aids home this morning."

"I think we gathered that bit of news, dad," Alvin chuckled.

Sylvia suppressed a laugh that almost escaped. "Well, it's good to see y'all."

She avoided Alvin's gaze as she attempted to walk around him.

Lightly touching her arm, he stopped her. "Hey, what made you come home so soon? Is everything alright?"

Her brown eyes narrowed at Alvin as she shifted her gaze from his hand to his face.

Was he really touching her arm after what Cordelia and the other lady had said? Where was Brinley?

She was probably waiting outside in her wedding dress.

The thought made Sylvia's scalp flare with heat.

Alvin removed his hand from her arm. "Sorry for touching you. I know I have no right. I wanted to make sure you're okay."

"No, I'm sorry. I don't know what's wrong with me today." Sylvia flat-out lied. Jealousy never did anyone a bit of good.

"No, I shouldn't have grabbed your arm," Alvin argued.

"It's alright." She looked down at the pew and back at Alvin. "Where's your girlfriend?"

"My what?" The look on Alvin's face couldn't have been more baffled if Sylvia had asked him if he'd been to the moon lately.

"You know. Brinley. Your girlfriend."

Alvin scrunched his eyebrows and swallowed before asking, "How do you even know about Brinley?"

"I met her at Breakwater here a while back." She said, resisting the urge to press on her rolling stomach.

He cocked his head, and a slight frown passed his lips. "Regardless, she's not my girlfriend. I can't imagine she would tell you differently."

"No, I assumed y'all were together after seeing how you two laughed and carried on last night." That sentence came out before she thought it through.

She stared at the carpet.

Wishing she could somehow fall through the floor to the basement.

That had to be more comfortable than this.

Alvin continued with his questions to figure out where Sylvia got her information. "How did you –"

His question got cut off by the topic of their conversation walking up. Hand in hand with another man.

"Thanks for inviting us here last night, Alvin."

Sylvia looked at the man and then Brinley before her eyes landed on Alvin. Brinley stuck her hand out. "Hi, Sylvia. Nice to see you here. This is my boyfriend, Darren."

BOYFRIEND! Now would be a good time for the floor to bust open. Any moment now.

"Ummm, nice to meet you, Darren," Sylvia mumbled before excusing herself to melt into the nearest pew.

Did Sylvia say the situation couldn't get any more awkward earlier?

Yeah, obviously, she was wrong.

# Chapter 36

With Keatyn at the wheel, the sleek pontoon boat cruised effortlessly out of the dock and into Pensacola Bay. It had enough space for ten people to move around comfortably, allowing the five passengers plenty of room to enjoy themselves.

Sylvia's cousin, Lisa, had come home with her parents to spend a few nights exploring Pensacola and the surrounding area.

The other passengers included Rebecca and Keatyn's college friend, Lucy. They each contributed $50 to rent the pontoon for four hours, aiming to enjoy a much-needed girls' day.

The upbeat rhythm of "Girls Just Want to Have Fun" filled the air, its lively melody competing with the joyful shouts and laughter of the women gathered on the boat. Laughter at Sylvia's expense.

She regretted sharing the embarrassing story of assuming Alvin and Brinley were together. It had slipped out during a moment of weakness.

After deciding to devise a plan to help Sylvia eat crow and win Alvin back, they all shared a good laugh.

They had a pontoon boat, a cooler filled with ice-cold water, snacks, chicken salad sandwiches, and chips for lunch. With their desire to have fun, that was all they needed, and they couldn't help but act like schoolgirls.

Lucy, Rebecca, and Lisa ended up at the front of the Pontoon, watching a dolphin putt on a show. Sylvia sat in the seat directly in front of the steering wheel.

Keatyn waved at people on a dolphin cruise before looking at Sylvia. "Why didn't you say something to him?"

Sylvia's eyes bugged out. "I was mortified."

Keatyn's lips flattened. "I'm not very happy you came to the house and didn't speak to me. If you'd called or texted, I would've told you all about Brinley and Darren."

"I know." Smashing her head into the plush headrest, Sylvia moaned. "Quit rubbing it in."

Raising both eyebrows, Keatyn glanced at Sylvia and then back at the water. "Alvin also said you've dodged his calls all week."

"Because I don't know what to say to him," Sylvia said into the pillow.

Sporting a smug expression, Keatyn leaned across the steering wheel. "How about saying you're sorry for acting like a goober, and you love him and will do anything to be my sister-in-law?"

Sylvia moved her head to the side, revealing a long red line across her cheek from the seam on the headrest. "I mean, why don't you tell me how you really feel?"

Pressing the back of her hand to her mouth, Keatyn cleared her throat before speaking. "You know I will."

The rest of their party made their way to the middle of the Pontoon. Steadily laughing over any and everything.

Lucy grabbed Keatyn's arm. "Did you see that dolphin? It was playing in the water, and it kept smiling at me. I think it loved me."

"Oh, I'm sure it did." Keatyn replied with one eyebrow raised.

Sylvia chewed on her bottom lip as she witnessed the exchange between Keatyn and Lucy.

Keatyn shared how she and Lucy were best friends in college and for years afterward. At least up until they clashed over a man. Keatyn dated Peter first, and he broke up with her before starting to date Lucy.

Keatyn had been so mad that she gave Lucy a hard time at the place they both worked, where Keatyn was the boss.

Lucy quit her job over Keatyn, and they didn't speak for months afterward. After Lucy and Peter married, Keatyn ended up apologizing to both Peter and Lucy for how she acted. They accepted, and now Keatyn and Lucy were friends again.

If they could be friends after all that, Alvin would forgive Sylvia.

Right?

Later that afternoon, Sylvia and Lisa drove down the scenic highway between Navarre and Pensacola beaches.

Lisa gasped and pulled her phone out to record the white sand and waves as they crept by at fifteen miles per hour. "This view is the bomb."

"Tell me about it. I'm considering buying a home on Navarre Beach this time."  Her lips parted in a lopsided grin. "That is if I can afford it."

Sylvia's phone buzzed, and Lisa read the message from Mom.

*We are having grilled burgers for dinner.*

Lisa tapped on the keyboard before turning her attention back to the view.

Sounds good

*Please bring tomatoes from Erma Dean's market*

Okie Dokie

*Be careful. Love u*

Love u 2

It only took thirty minutes to reach the Farmer's Market between Gulf Breeze and Pensacola.

One of the owners, Clara Dean Shaw, greeted them. "Good afternoon, Sylvia."

"Hi, Clara Dean. This is my cousin, Lisa. She's visiting from Georgia."

"Hello, Lisa."

Before leaving the market, they picked out five ripe tomatoes, cantaloupe, and some peaches.

On the road to Milton, Sylvia's phone buzzed again. Lisa read the message.

*It's Alvin. Wanted you to know I got a new phone. I've called you three times this week. You okay?*

Sylvia told her what to type.

I'm good. Just embarrassed.

No need to be embarrassed. Could it be you're jealous?

Lisa sucked a breath in. "Do you want to pull over? I feel like I'm intruding reading these messages."
"No, it's fine. I'd tell you anyway."
Lisa typed what Sylvia dictated.

Maybe I am.

Now we're getting somewhere! Let's meet up to talk.

Ok

Wanna talk things through tomorrow?

Yes

Perfect. See you tomorrow. Have a good night.

You too

Lisa laid the phone down and giggled. "Looks like things may work out with you and handsome, after all."

A burst of giggles came from Sylvia, and she gave Lisa the eye. "Handsome, is it?"

Lisa snickered. "Hey! I call 'em like I see "em."

A million butterflies danced around in Sylvia's stomach the entire drive home.

# Chapter 37

Gareth Davenport's voice resonated through-out the auditorium. "As I've mentioned, preaching is a serious responsibility. So, why do I strive to be the best preacher I can be?"

"First and foremost, I preach every sermon to myself. If it resonates with others, that's just an added bonus. I want to hear uplifting and soul-nourishing sermons whenever I worship on the Lord's Day. After all, I am a Christian first and a preacher second."

A sudden blast from a car horn made Sylvia flinch in her seat. Several church members glanced around, as if they were reprimanding the driver for the noise.

Gareth remained unfazed as he continued with his sermon. "Most of my knowledge comes from Bible classes and personal study in preparation for sermons. This is why we emphasize the importance of attending Bible classes and engaging in individual studies."

"In Bible class, we encourage and uplift one another, sharing knowledge and insights. Bible classes should inspire us to ask questions, study diligently, and meditate on God's word. We should take what we have learned and share it with others."

"And sermons should cause us to reflect on our own lives, follow along in our Bibles, and make sure what is being taught and said is the truth. And if we find it true according to God's word, it should cause us to adjust in our lives as needed."

"So, why do I want to be the best preacher I can be? Because I am the preacher, my wife and children will hear most in their lives. My wife placed great confidence in me as her husband and preacher for the rest of our lives together. And I do not want to short-change her, our family, or anyone else."

Gareth looked across the pews until his eyes landed on Keatyn. "She should not be subjected to poorly prepared, shoddy preaching or false teaching because she loves me and married me. I want to be the best preacher I can be to help her, and our kids go to heaven. You can't lead where you refuse to go, and you can't teach others what you don't know."

Sylvia surveyed the people sitting on the pew with her, and her heart soared. Tying in the sermon to her last year of life, she reflected on all the changes.

She never would've believed her parents would step foot in a church building. Yet, there they sat, listening to a sermon.

If Sylvia had refused Keatyn's invitation to come to church, they would not be there right now. She couldn't lead where she refused to go. Gareth was one hundred percent correct.

They were there, even though Dad had on a dirty shirt.

Even though they barely arrived before the morning sermon due to a blowout on the way. Her dad's Suburban had a nail embedded in the tire.

That nail caused them to miss Bible class and the singing before the sermon. A State Trooper pulled over and helped her dad change the tire.

What a blessing he'd been.

That nail almost kept her family out of worship.

Almost.

Sylvia couldn't help comparing the nail she had in her purse's side pocket to the nails that pierced Jesus on the cross.

Whereas the nail in the tire almost kept them from church, the nails that pierced Jesus allowed people, including her family, the possibility of a home in Heaven.

Sylvia only had one issue she had to fix. Alvin. And he just walked out of the church building.

After church, Dad pulled over in front of Vine's, one of Pensacola's fanciest restaurants. He glanced at Sylvia, "Hop out."

Screwing her face into a question, Sylvia leaned close to the driver's seat. "Why?"

"Don't question your dad. Go on in there and ask for a table." Mom gave Sylvia one of her famous mom looks.

"Oh. I didn't know we were eating lunch here. I hope y'all are buying." She gripped Lisa's arm. "Come on, you can go with me to get a table."

Lisa shriveled away from Sylvia. "You go ahead." She pulled her phone out of her purse. "I have to make a call."

She peeked at the third row. "Rhyland? Oakland? Wanna come in with your mama?"

"Nope," Rhyland said while Oakland shook his head.

Sylvia stuck her tongue out at everyone in the vehicle before hopping out, shaking her head.

Marching up the steps to the historic home turned restaurant, Sylvia tucked her white shirt in the front of her plaid pants.

The hostess standing behind the podium flashed a smile. "Welcome to Vines. How many in your party?"

Alvin stepped out of the first room on the right and smiled at the hostess. "Just us two."

Sylvia's head snapped in his direction, with her mouth gaping open. A squeak slipped out, and she swallowed.

Alvin grabbed Sylvia's hand and led her into the room he'd left. She stopped in her tracks and gripped Alvin's arm, causing him to stop with her.

The special occasions room was dimly lit with candles placed all over, with three on the single dining table. The gold and black striped wallpaper had purple flowers in such random places it flowed perfectly with the ornate furniture.

Tears glimmered across her eyelids, and she loosened her grip on Alvin's arm. "What's this?"

"This is me hijacking you for our first date," Alvin said as he pulled a chair out for her.

She took the seat and met Alvin's tender gaze. "But how?"

A grin passed Alvin's lips, and he jiggled his eyebrows. "Your mama loves me."

Her eyes sparkled, and she shrugged. "You're not wrong."

"What about her daughter?" His breath tingled in her ear as his words came out so softly she had to turn her head to focus on his lips.

Which was a mistake. The air left her lungs, and she matched his tone. "What do you mean?"

His penetrating gaze dared her to look away. "Is there a chance you have feelings for me?"

Scarlet flames warmed her cheeks. "Yes, and I don't know how much longer I can keep pretending I don't."

"That's all I've wanted." Sylvia almost felt Alvin's heart banging in his chest as he leaned closer. "A chance."

After everything they'd been through, could this really be happening?

Alvin had been the one constant in her life since Lee's faked death. The one person who made her laugh when she wanted to cry.

But he was also the one she pushed away with all her might. Could it be the kidnapping made her heart more open to love?

Alvin's lips hovered just above hers as he paused, the scent of sweet cherries lingering in the air as his breath mingled with hers. His gaze remained fixed on her face, and a feeling of weightlessness shivered through Sylvia.

Her mind turned to mush as she tilted her face up to meet Alvin's, ready for the kiss she had waited her whole life for.

# Chapter 38

Sunlight streamed through the windows as Keatyn carried a tray with four cups of coffee to the living room. She handed Sylvia a cup. "We can head out after we drink our coffee."

"Sounds good." Sylvia licked her lips with a sip of the homemade White Chocolate Mocha. "You know I don't like any of the sweet stuff but yours."

"My wife makes the best coffee," Gareth added as he stepped into the living room, claiming his coffee and kissing Keatyn's forehead. "Where's Alvin?"

"He had to step outside to make a call. He shouldn't be long."

Gareth checked his watch. "We have to pick Myles and Rodney up in an hour."

Rolling her eyes, Keatyn chuckled. "I can't believe they've roped you into flea marketing with them."

Gareth pulled Keatyn close to his side. "It's fun. We find all types of interesting things."

"Y'all should come with us instead of parasailing," Alvin commented as he lumbered in from the patio.

"Nope. We're both looking forward to our day." Sylvia replied.

A couple of hours later, Sylvia and Keatyn boarded the boat after dropping out of the sky on their second annual parasailing adventure.

They had almost reached the shore when Blank, the boat driver, pointed at a plane. "What's that say? It's not normal for planes to advertise in September."

Sylvia's eyes followed his, and her heart flipped in her chest. Does that say what I think it does?

Marry me, Sylvia, flapped in the wind behind the plane.

With her eyes on the sky, Sylvia grabbed Keatyn's arm. "Is that for me?"

Keatyn grinned and nodded.

Sylvia's heart slammed into her chest. "I don't know what to say."

The boat glided to a stop, and Sylvia stood up.

Before she could get out of the boat, her eyes landed on those closest to her at the shore.

Rhyland and Oakland held bouquets of flowers while Dad and Myles each had their phones raised.

Mom and Cordelia reminded her of the boys when they mocked one another. They both stood, hands clasped under their chins and smiles glued to their faces.

Alvin helped Sylvia off the boat before dropping to one knee at the water's edge.

His eyes caressed her. "Sylvia Diane Engle Mason, will you marry me?"

Dropping into the water beside Alvin, Sylvia leaned her forehead against his. "Yes. Without a doubt, yes!"

The family gave them a few minutes before going in for hugs.

"I can't believe you had an airplane proposal." Sylvia giggled. "I bet marriage with you will never be dull."

Alvin raised out of the water and spun Sylvia around. "You have no idea."

"Rodney and Tanya are at the house firing up the grill. Who's hungry?" Gareth asked.

Sylvia raised her hand. "I am."

As she lowered her hand, she gasped. The ring took her breath away with its oval shape, a center-cut diamond with three layers of sapphires wrapped around it. "Alvin?"

He raised her hand to his lips. "Yes?"

"Where'd you get this ring?" She'd never let him spend that much money on a ring.

"It's a family heirloom."

Her eyes bugged out. "Then Keatyn should have it."

"Oh no," Keatyn added her two cents. "That ring has always been meant for Alvin's wife. For you, my soon to be sister-in-law."

Sylvia leaned her head on Keatyn's forearm, unable to reach her shoulder. "I sure love my soon to be sister-in-law."

"I love you, too." Keatyn cocked her head to lay on top of Sylvia's. "Ready to go? I heard there's some shrimp on the grill."

"Absolutely."

# Chapter 39



## SIX MONTHS LATER

S now-capped mountains, trees, and cabins. That's what Sylvia called the view of a lifetime. She only had two days until her dream wedding. Even though the road to get there had been rocky, she wouldn't complain. The Lord had blessed her more than she could imagine.

Antonio Morales had made a deal to testify for the prosecution in exchange for protection. He was allowed to call Sylvia before leaving. He'd cried and begged her to forgive him. Even though it was hard, she'd granted the forgiveness he asked for.

His nasty daughter, Kemena, had been captured in a penthouse suite in Nassau. She was now awaiting trial for more things than Sylvia could name.

A letter from Louise arrived before they left for Fairbanks, Alaska. Sylvia opened the envelope with trembling hands.

Dear Sylvia,

I can do nothing to make things right for what we did to you, but I must at least explain.

My husband, Nicholas, needed a kidney from our son, Angel, who is in a Cuban prison.

Mr. Morales promised to get Nicholas the transplant if we helped him. He said you were Evangeline, and you had lost your senses. When I realized you were not, I tried to make things right.

My son, Manuel, knew the circumstances, and he accepts responsibility. He begs you to forgive him. I beg the same.

My Nicholas lost his battle with kidney disease, and my Angel still rots in the Cuban prison. This is my punishment for what I did.

Manuel is in prison here in Florida and I live in a town called Crestview in the women's shelter.

I have no money or way to get home to Cuba. I couldn't help my Angel even if I had the money.

Please live your life as the joyful person I found you to be and put this behind you.

Begging your forgiveness,<br>Louise Estrada

Sylvia rubbed her arms as she stepped off the balcony and into the cabin, wrapping a fluffy blanket around her body.

Her parents had rented two cabins, one for the ladies with enough bunk beds for everyone, and another for the men.

Handing her a cup of cocoa, Keatyn grinned. "Cold out there, huh?"

Sylvia blew the cocoa before taking a sip. "Cold but gorgeous."

"Are you not happy with your choice of wedding destinations?" Keatyn put her hands on Sylvia's shoulders. "You look distraught. Is everything okay?"

"I'm one hundred percent happy with Alaska." Sylvia's eyes turned dreamy as she took in the view through the glass doors. "I've always wanted an Alaskan winter wedding."

Following Sylvia's gaze, Keatyn shrugged. "It is definitely breathtaking." She sipped her cocoa. "Then what's wrong?"

Handing Keatyn the letter, Sylvia sat on the sofa closest to the fireplace. The room held two sofas, a couple of chairs by the fireplace, and bunk beds.

After reading the letter, Keatyn probed Sylvia's eyes. "Ahh, I see. Does this not bring you closure?"

"How could it when I know Louise has no one to help her?" Sylvia twisted her engagement ring. "She helped me after she figured out I wasn't Evangeline. She has a good heart."

"Okay. Then let's talk to Gareth and Alvin about helping her. Surely we can do something to get her into a home and meet her daily needs." Keatyn bit her lip. "If that's what you want."

Sylvia shot off the sofa. "It is."

Keatyn laughed. "It's settled, then. Not to change the subject, but I can't tell you how excited Gareth is to perform the wedding."

Sylvia raised a brow before taking another sip of her cocoa. "First wedding in Alaska, I take it?"

Keatyn screwed her face up. "Not at all. I think this is the fifth one since we married."

Sylvia plopped Keatyn across the head with a pillow. "You're so funny. You should quit your VP job and become a stand-up comedian."

Keatyn tried to duck the pillow but failed. "You sound like Rebecca."

"Well, she's right." Sylvia dropped the pillow to her side. "I hate that she and Kyle couldn't come."

"She was bummed out big time. But her family had been planning their big reunion in Orlando for almost a year."

Sylvia pouted, "I know, but I still hate it."

The door thudded closed. Lisa barreled into the cabin, followed by Brinley. "This place is stunning."

"I agree with that statement." Brinley added. "Thank you for allowing me to come with Darren. I wasn't sure you'd want me here."

"Why wouldn't I?" Understanding flashed across Sylvia's face. "Oh. Do you think I'm upset you went on a couple dates with Alvin? Not at all. As a matter of fact, I owe you a thank you for kicking me into gear with your talk."

"That's a relief. I think things worked out like they were supposed to. Without Alvin, I wouldn't have met Darren."

Cordelia and a few other ladies ambled up behind Brinley and Lisa. "HAS ANYONE SEEN MY HEARING AIDS?" Cordelia's loud voice nearly busted their eardrums.

Keatyn pulled the covers back on Cordelia's bunk bed. "I found them."

Tanya wagged her finger at Cordelia. "I told you they were probably in your bed."

Cordelia turned toward Tanya. "DID YOU SAY SOMETHING, DEAR?"

Laughter erupted from everyone but Cordelia. She put in the hearing aids and stood with her hand on her hip. "What's so funny?"

Lily wrapped her arms around Cordelia. "You're funny, Grandma."

Her eyes softened, and she hugged Lily to her legs. "I guess I am, sweetheart."

# Chapter 40

Joy swelled in Sylvia's heart as she breathed in the scent of fresh crisp snow. She couldn't believe she finally had her winter wedding.

Her eyes crinkled with a smile as she took in the setting. Twelve white chairs, each tied with luxurious red satin bows, lined both sides of the aisle. Between the chairs, a soft carpet of velvety crimson rose petals sprawled out, their vibrant color strikingly contrasted against the pure, glistening white of the snow. Each petal seemed to shimmer in the sunlight, creating a dreamlike pathway.

In the distance, an awe-inspiring backdrop of towering snow-capped mountains stood majestically, their rugged silhouettes framed against a clear azure sky, serving as the perfect, breathtaking setting for the occasion.

This serene winter wonderland, with its natural beauty and elegant details, set the stage for a truly unforgettable wedding.

Her wedding!

She ran her hand down the white gown that cascaded to her feet. Her late grandmother's white mink coat fell to her knees and complemented the dress perfectly. She wore her hair in ringlets down her back, with a simple tiara tucked into the crown of her head.

She pressed her small frame against Daddy's sturdy arm, thankful to have him there as they waited on their turn to navigate the bright aisle. Ahead of them, Keatyn and Lisa glided gracefully in their flowing red bridesmaid gowns, the fabric shimmering softly with each step.

Moisture welled up on her lashes as she held her gaze steady on Alvin's captivating eyes. Each heartbeat thrummed in her chest, echoing the exhilaration that coursed through her veins at the sight of his warm, beaming smile.

It was as if time stood still, and in that precious moment, a world of possibilities unfurled before her. She envisioned their future together, filled with love, laughter, and shared dreams, and her heart swelled with an eager longing to finally become his wife.

Walking down the aisle passed as if in a dream. Daddy kissed her cheek before taking his place beside Mom.

Gareth cleared his throat, his gaze landing on Alvin first then Sylvia. "Who gives this woman to be wed?"

Dad, Mom, Rhyland, and Oakland all stood together and said in unison, with Oakland's loud scream nearly drowning out the others, "We do."

"Is there anyone here that has a valid reason why these two cannot lawfully be joined in marriage?"

"Nope!" Rhyland shouted before dropping down onto his chair. Laughter erupted from the guests.

Gareth grinned as the rest of Sylvia's family took their seats. "But from the beginning of the creation, God made them male and female. For this reason, a man shall leave his father and mother and be joined to his wife, and the two shall become one flesh, so then they are no longer two, but one flesh. Therefore, what God has joined together, let not man separate. Mark 10:6-9."

"In a few moments, you two will become one flesh. Sylvia and Alvin, I thank the Lord that you have found each other, and I am truly grateful to have you both as part of my family."

Alvin took Sylvia's hand in his, their fingers intertwining as he gazed deeply into her eyes. The warmth of his touch sent a shiver of electricity through her, and in that moment, it felt as though time stood still.

Gareth cleared his throat and stated, "1 Corinthians 13:1-13 is a powerful reminder that without love, we are nothing."

*"Though I speak with the tongues of men and of angels, but have not love, I have become sounding brass or a clanging cymbal. And though I have the gift of prophecy, and understand all mysteries and all knowledge, and though I have all faith, so that I could remove mountains, but have not love, I am nothing. And though I bestow all my goods to feed the poor, and though I give my body to be burned, but have not love, it profits me nothing. Love suffers long and is kind; love does not envy; love does not parade itself, is not puffed up; does not behave rudely, does not seek its own, is not provoked, thinks no evil; does not rejoice in iniquity, but rejoices in the truth; bears all things, believes all things, hopes all things, endures all things. Love never fails. But whether there are prophecies, they will fail; whether there are tongues, they will cease; whether there is knowledge, it will vanish away. For we know in part and we prophesy in part. But when that which is perfect has come, then that which is in part will be done away. When I was a child, I spoke as a child, I understood as a child, I thought as a child; but when I became a man, I put away childish things. For now we see in a mirror, dimly, but then face to face. Now I know in part, but then I shall know just as I also am known. And now abide faith, hope, love, these three; but the greatest of these is love."*

After delivering his wedding sermon, Gareth turned to Alvin. "Alvin, do you take Sylvia to be your lawfully wedded wife? Will you love her, comfort her, and keep her? Will you forsake all others and remain faithful to her for as long as you both shall live?"

When her eyes met Alvin's, she saw beauty, love, and life. His gaze pierced into hers as if he would never love anyone else as he loved her in that moment.

Alvin's voice came out husky. "I will."

"Will you, Sylvia take Alvin to be your lawfully wedded husband? Will you love and comfort and obey him, and forsake all others and remain faithful to him as long as you live?"

Sylvia raised her head a notch to meet Alvin's eyes. His light brown tuxedo and matching brown snow boots didn't phase her. She would marry him if he wore sweatpants and a hoodie. To her, Alvin was the man God had intended for her. Her soul mate. "A bazillion times over, I will."

"By the power vested in me given by the state of Alaska, I now pronounce you husband and wife." Alvin shot Gareth an impatient glare when he paused. Gareth grinned before continuing. "Alvin, for the first time, you may kiss your wife."

Alvin lifted Sylvia and kissed her for everyone to see. Her silver, sparkly Uggs peeked out from beneath her dress, prompting a squeal and clap from Lily.

Oakland and Rhyland both stuck their tongues out. "Gross," Rhyland exclaimed.

Sylvia and Alvin stood in amazed silence as the Northern Lights danced across the sky several hours later. They had booked a dog-sledding tour, hoping to catch a glimpse of the Northern Lights, followed by an Alaskan dinner served in a warm yurt.

Alvin had promised Sylvia a guided hiking trip up the mountain. She had pinched herself more than once since their wedding. Today felt like a dream.

Alvin wrapped his arms around Sylvia. "I love you so much."

Sylvia leaned into his embrace. "I love you, Alvin." She tilted her head to look into his eyes. "I will never leave you."

Kissing the top of her head, he sighed. "I know that."

"Thank you for waiting so long for me."

He lightly squeezed her. "I studied the book of Job a lot." That earned him a jab in the ribs, and he snickered. "No, seriously, I hope you know I would've waited as long as you needed. I'm convinced we're meant to be."

He lifted her hand to his lips and pressed a feather kiss on her wrist.

"'As am I," she replied, her voice barely above a whisper. She turned her face toward his, her warm breath mingling with the cool air between them. Gently, she ran her fingers down the side of his cheek, her touch tender and lingering, as if to communicate her longing without words.

A wide grin broke across his face, lighting up his features. With a soft chuckle, he leaned forward, closing the distance, and met her lips with his own. Sylvia savored the sweetness of the moment as their worlds aligned in the warmth of the kiss.

# *Epilogue*

Life in Pensacola couldn't be better if you asked Sylvia. Not allowing the past to destroy her future had been the best decision she'd ever made. There were hard days, but she had the Lord and her husband to lean upon when fear threatened to creep in.

Even after six months of marriage, she and Alvin were as happy as the day they said their vows. Even more so. Alvin had officially started attending Preaching School, and Sylvia was back in the office as Prosecutor.

The boys had settled in nicely with Alvin. They spent time together, and the boys seemed to be happy. Rhyland still called Alvin by his name, but Oakland had called him daddy the other night after Alvin tucked them in for bed.

Alvin had almost floated out of their bedroom to tell her the news.

"See that?" The Ultrasound Technician, Layla Simmons, pointed at the screen, snapping Sylvia out of her own head. "There's the baby."

The need to scream for joy surged within Sylvia, but she held back. She didn't want the hospital staff to think she was unfit to raise a child. Instead, she squeezed Alvin's hand.

Alvin's eyes filled with tears as he stared at the screen. "Everything seems okay? She's fine, right?"

Raising her eyebrows, Sylvia squeezed his hand back. "She? So, you want a girl?"

Alvin grinned at Sylvia. "I'll be happy with either. But we already have two boys. And I thought you'd want a girl."

She cocked her head and raised her shoulder. "I do want a girl. But like you said, I'll be happy with either."

Layla smiled, "You only have around six months to wait."

Six months would fly by, and they'd be a family of five. Sylvia could hardly believe it. Her journey had plenty of bumps along the way, but they'd led her to this point in her life.

A wife. A mom. But most importantly, a Christian.

Thank you for taking the time to read **Sylvia's Journey**. If you found it enjoyable, I would be grateful if you could leave a review. Your feedback truly makes a difference!

# acknowledgements

Writing the second book in our Seeds of Faith series has been a joy. To be able to remember my late brother, Alvin, in such a way has brought me both laughter and tears.

To the real Sylvia - I imagine someone like you would have been a perfect fit for Alvin! He was funny yet profound. Loving, yet complex. He was someone I'm proud to call my brother. Just as you are someone I'm pleased to call my friend.

Cassidy - there's no one else I would've wanted on the cover. You have a glow that I've always loved, and I'm thankful you're my daughter!

Shelby with SMB Photography never disappoints. She takes the most perfect shots that flow so well with my stories!

To my ARC readers, thank you a million times for reading my stories and giving feedback.

Thank you to Vickie for reading my proof and coming up with "Betrayals & Beginnings" - it flows so well with the story.

My honey, Mark, is such a gem for continuing to grant me full access to his library of sermons. He preaches from the heart, and I'm so glad he's mine!

To the person who proofread and provided such fantastic feedback, WOW!  Stephanie, you helped me see things through a reader's eyes, and I'm very grateful. You made Sylvia's Journey flow so much better!

Dear readers, thank you from the bottom of my heart. I appreciate your support! Please stay tuned as we continue this series with many journeys.

XOXO

# about the author

Leah Brewer is a multi-genre author who focuses on writing clean books that anyone can read. She was born and raised in Des Arc, Arkansas, before moving to Northeast Arkansas when her children were young.

She spends her spare time with her husband, Mark, their grown children, and granddaughter, Charlotte. If she's not on a beach, she's dreaming about when she can be!

# Preview

Keep reading for a preview of the next installment in this captivating series. This Christmas story, titled "Frankie's Journey," promises to take you on an enchanting adventure filled with holiday spirit, heartwarming moments, and unforgettable characters. Discover what awaits Frankie as she embarks on a journey that will change her life forever during the most magical time of the year.

# Chapter 1

Death had been the one constant in Frankie Kingston's life. Now that she had no one left, would she be next? Or would she spend her days dreaming of what should be? Walking around that big house alone?

She rubbed her hands down the sleeves of her black sweater dress and sighed. The Haven of Rest Cemetery was the last place she wanted to be. How could she get through another funeral? She clutched at her chest, trying to hold the sobs inside.

When all else failed, she could count on death to rear its ugly head.

Her entire being seemed to move in slow motion yet spin simultaneously as she gripped the side of the casket.

Leaning close to his ear, she swallowed the lump in her throat before whispering, "I love you, Daddy-o, and I'm forever your baby girl."

A strand of curly dark brown hair fell onto the pillow beside Daddy when she rose. She picked it up, the wind caught it, and it floated away. Her gaze stayed glued to that lone hair strand until it disappeared. She couldn't help but compare it to Daddy. Just like the hair, he was gone. She could do nothing to change it, like fighting against the wind.

She rubbed her pale fingers down the fabric on Daddy's favorite purple silk tie and hung her head. This would be the last time she ever touched it. The last time she'd see his face.

She wanted so badly for him to be here still. But his life on earth was over. She had no choice but to face it.

A chilly early morning breeze nipped at her cheeks, and she shivered. Maybe it was from more than the cold. Seeing Daddy finally at peace caused mixed emotions. Sadness for her sake but happy he had no more pain.

After laying a letter she'd written beneath his tie, she gave Daddy one last look before settling into one of the seats reserved for the family. No family would be coming, though. She was the last. And her best friend had texted she couldn't make it, either.

Angie Patterson, Frankie's coworker from The Lily Pad Boutique, pulled up. Frankie bestowed a half smile on her and Jessica Glaze, the other team member, when they made it across the graveyard. The owner had left on a tour of Europe the day before Daddy lost his battle.

They wrapped Frankie in a group hug. "We're opening an hour late so that we can be here for you," Jessica mumbled in Frankie's ear.

Other than her work family, a few of Daddy's friends, some church members, his attorney, and three partners from the firm where he worked sat scattered around her, but that was it. George Owens, the Rest Easy Funeral Home Director, glanced from the sky to the preacher. He must be praying the rain would hold off until after the funeral.

The preacher, David Love, stood at the end of the casket. "Larry Kingston was a good man who fought hard. He passed from this life on March 14, at home with his daughter Frances Mary Kingston by his side. Larry was preceded in death by his parents, William and Estelle Kingston, and his loving wife, Helen."

Frankie wiped her face with a tissue as her vision blurred. She was the only surviving relative. She'd never wished so hard for a brother or sister. Someone she could lean on for comfort. A distant cousin, even.

Over an hour later, Frankie sat alone on a cold, hard bench, listening to thunder rumble in the distance. She fought the urge to laugh hysterically when the first raindrop hit her hand. Since her ride had already left, she'd have to make the trek home in the rain on foot. Daddy's attorney, Simon Wheeler, hadn't wanted to leave her, but she'd insisted. She desperately needed more time to say goodbye to Daddy.

Her eyes lingered on Mama's side of the double headstone. "Daddy's with you now, Mama. I love you both so much."

A blaring car horn snapped Frankie out of the trance she'd allowed herself to fall into. She covered her eyes to block out the rain and waved at Melody Rodgers.

Melody opened her umbrella and hurried across the grass, the bottoms of her black scrubs soaking wet. "Are you trying to make yourself sick out here in the cold rain?" She sat next to Frankie, holding the umbrella over them both. "Look at yourself. You're drenched."

Frankie brought a trembling hand to her face and rubbed water out of her eyes. "I'm sorry. You're right. I shouldn't be out here."

Melody pressed her full lips together and exhaled. "No, I'm sorry. I shouldn't be getting on to you today of all days. I know you're upset, and I wasn't here for you. The ambulance brought several people to the ER after a major car accident. It took a few hours to help the surgeon finish up. Raines is still there. I'm so sorry, Frankie."

Frankie shrugged. "It's not like you caused the wreck. You had to try to save lives. It's what you and Raines do. I'm so glad y'all found one another."

Melody held her hand out, raindrops glistening on her bronze skin. "Come on, let's get you some dry clothes."

Frankie dropped her head a second before raising it to stare at the fresh mound of dirt. "What am

I going to do now? No parents or family to speak of, and I'm not even twenty-four years old. Without Daddy, I feel so alone. I already miss him so much."

Melody lowered herself onto the wet bench and hugged Frankie close. "You'll never be alone as long as I'm alive."

Frankie laid her head on Melody's shoulder and stared at Daddy's final resting place. "Thank you for being here for me."

"Always."

Despite the cold rain and sopping wet clothes, they sat on the bench for another few minutes before running to Melody's car.

# Chapter 2

"Daddy did what?" Frankie stared at Simon Wheeler with her mouth gaping open. A fluttery tingling struck her belly. "Did you say he bought a camp for orphans?"

Frankie never dreamed the meeting with Daddy's attorney would turn out like this.

Glancing around the room, she attempted to keep a neutral expression. The only thing that helped was focusing on a painting of an old barn surrounded by rolling hills hanging behind the attorney.

Simon Wheeler patted her hand. The turquoise ring in the shape of a bird brought Frankie's attention to his index finger. Simon had always been a quirky man, but Daddy touted him as the best attorney in the state. "Not specifically for them, but to help give them a purpose during the holidays. You know he always had a soft spot for the Children's Home there in Pensacola."

"Yes, I know." She steadily shook her head. "Daddy did, but that has nothing to do with me."

Simon cocked his head, and a piece of graying hair fell into his face. He smoothed it back into place and creased his forehead. "It may not have then, but it does now."

Jerking her gaze from the painting, she stared head-on at Simon. "Why do you say that?"

Simon swiveled his light orange leather chair around and clicked a button on the TV screen. "I think it'll be better for you to hear it from Larry."

Daddy appeared on the screen with a head full of dark hair and color on his face. He must've made the video soon after being given six months to live. His brown eyes implored her to listen from the screen.

"Hello, my sweet Frances. I hope you don't get too mad at me for my actions." He paused and rubbed his eyes.

"Pensacola has always held a piece of my heart, and you know I was an orphan until my parents adopted me. I want to do something for the kids at the Pensacola Children's Home who haven't been adopted. Something more than writing a check for clothes or food."

"This is why I bought the camp. I planned to fix it up. I even started on it before I got sick. But alas, that was not to be. Frances, please pick up where I left off. Fix the place up and hold a Christmas Festival where the kids can run booths and be hands-on.

Let's give them something to do other than get into trouble."

"I'm sorry I never said anything to you. I didn't know how since you stopped enjoying Christmas. I planned to take you there before I got sick. Even though you probably have reservations about this, I know you'll do the right thing. I can see you giving the kids a bit of happiness, and I'm confident you'll also get a bit of joy back." His brown eyes seemed to sparkle like he knew a secret that Frankie didn't.

"You have the best heart out of anyone I know. Please do as I ask. I beg you. Go there yourself and do what you can for those kids. There's help waiting for you at the house in Pensacola. I love you. You were the one thing I knew I did right. My pride and joy, my baby girl."

The sly grin Frankie knew all too well appeared on his face. "Oh, and before I forget, take good care of my car. Drive the wheels off it and do so knowing I've gotten more than one smile, picturing you finally getting to drive it around. I wholeheartedly approve!"

"I pray you'll learn to love the Lord with your whole heart. Don't wait too late. I expect you to meet your mama and me in Heaven one day. Until then, take care."

Frankie sat stunned for a few minutes, letting what he said sink in.

Simon cleared his throat. "Listen, I know this is a lot. Do you need some time to think about it?"

Itching to peel off all her fingernails, she stuffed both hands underneath her legs to avoid leaving the office with nubs. How could Daddy ask her to do such a thing? "So, what happens if I say no? Do I sell the property?"

Smoothing the papers on his desk, Simon's voice came out steady and firm. "Not exactly. Suppose you decline to take the property on, as your father requested. In that case, it will be given to the second person in line."

Frankie cocked her head and screwed her lips up. "Who is that?"

Simon shrugged. "I'm not at liberty to discuss that just yet, but you'll still get your inheritance on top of his life insurance."

Frankie's brow furrowed. "That's not what it's about. I'm not worried about money, Simon. Who else could Daddy have left something to? We don't have any family left."

Simon shrugged again but didn't say anything. Silence closed in on them while Frankie pondered her next move. Daddy had always taught her to think before speaking, especially when upset.

She leaned forward, attempting to see if she could see any other names in the papers. Simon raised a brow as he stacked the papers and slipped them inside his briefcase. She inwardly groaned. Simon might be pushing seventy-something, but he was still alert as ever. "Can I stop by in the morning? That'll give me some time to think about what I want to do."

He laid the briefcase on the desk and tapped his fingers across it. His little half-smile seemed to dare her to grab it. "What's your first inclination?"

She tore her gaze away from the briefcase and met his eyes. "Honestly, as bad as I want to run out of this office and never look back, I can't. I probably should move to Pensacola and do what Daddy asked. For him. But Arkansas is my home, not Florida."

"I've been your daddy's friend for over thirty years, and I know he asked you to do this for a reason. Maybe you should listen to your heart and not your head."

Yeah, if only Frankie liked kids.